M000192087

MONDEGREEN

Ukrainian Research Institute
Harvard University

Harvard Library of Ukrainian Literature 2

HURI Editorial Board

Michael S. Flier
George G. Grabowicz
Oleh Kotsyuba, *Manager of Publications*
Serhii Plokhy, *Chairman*

Cambridge, Massachusetts

Volodymyr Rafeyenko

Mondegreen

Songs about Death and Love

LIBRARY OF
CONGRESS
SURPLUS
DUPLICATE

Translated and introduced by
Mark Andryczyk

Distributed by Harvard University Press
for the Ukrainian Research Institute
Harvard University

The Harvard Ukrainian Research Institute was established in 1973 as an integral part of Harvard University. It supports research associates and visiting scholars who are engaged in projects concerned with all aspects of Ukrainian studies. The Institute also works in close cooperation with the Committee on Ukrainian Studies, which supervises and coordinates the teaching of Ukrainian history, language, and literature at Harvard University.

© 2022 by the President and Fellows of Harvard College

All rights reserved
Printed in the U.S. on acid-free paper

ISBN 9780674275577 (hardcover), 9780674271708 (paperback), 9780674271746 (epub), 9780674271760 (PDF)

Library of Congress Control Number: 2021949032
LC record available at https://lccn.loc.gov/2021949032

Photo of Volodymyr Rafeyenko courtesy of Nataliia Kravchuk
Cover image and book design by
Mykola Leonovych, https://smalta.pro

Publication of this book has been made possible by the Ukrainian Research Institute Fund and the generous support of publications in Ukrainian studies at Harvard University by the following benefactors:

Ostap and Ursula Balaban	Irena Lubchak
Jaroslaw and Olha Duzey	Dr. Evhen Omelsky
Vladimir Jurkowsky	Eugene and Nila Steckiw
Myroslav and Irene Koltunik	Dr. Omeljan and
Damian Korduba Family	Iryna Wolynec
Peter and Emily Kulyk	Wasyl and Natalia Yerega

You can support our work of publishing academic books and translations of Ukrainian literature and documents by making a tax-deductible donation in any amount, or by including HURI in your estate planning. To find out more, please visit https://huri.harvard.edu/give.

The publication of this book was made possible, in part, by the Translate Ukraine Translation Program of the Ukrainian Book Institute (Ukraine).

The purchase of rights and preparation of translation were also supported by generous contributions from individual donors through a crowdfunding campaign organized by Razom for Ukraine (United States).

COLUMBIA | HARRIMAN INSTITUTE
Russian, Eurasian, and East European Studies

Publication of this book was made possible, in part, by a grant from the Harriman Institute, Columbia University.

We are deeply grateful for the generous support that this translation has received from the participants of the crowdfunding campaign organized by Razom for Ukraine. It is because of the patronage of visionary individuals such as these that the Ukrainian Research Institute at Harvard has been able to implement its sprawling programs in research and publications dedicated to the promotion of knowledge of Ukraine, its history, and culture. Thank you!

BENEFACTOR

Sviatoslav Bozhenko

CHAMPIONS

Yuriy Barminov

Chopivsky Family
Foundation

Oksana Falenchuk

Maria Genkin

Nadia Lubchenko

Tanya Nesterchuk

PATRONS

Natalia Bruslanova

Irena Chalupa

Nick Colby

Reilly Costigan-Humes

Kristy Davis

Anna Filonenko

Kateryna Iavorska

Alexandra Karaev

Oleh Kotsyuba

Alexey Ladokhin

Dr. Oleksandr Makeyev

Andrea Odezynska

Olga Onishchenko

Kirill Prokopenko

Nina Sakun

Katerina Semida Manoff

Tamara Shevchenko

Ania Solovei

Alexandre Starinsky

Kate Tsurkan

Olena Urmey

FRIENDS

Our gratitude also goes out to over thirty further friends of Razom for Ukraine and HURI who supported this publication with their donations.

All names are sorted by last name within each category of support.

Contents

Introduction

Linguistic Repositioning in a Time of War

Mark Andryczyk

"It's a valuable thing—the Kama Sutra in a time of war."
   —Volodymyr Rafeyenko, *Mondegreen: Songs about Death and Love*

In Volodymyr Rafeyenko's wartime novel *Mondegreen: Songs about Death and Love*, the author carves out an extraordinary space in which a writer can newly encounter his principal tool and closest companion—language. In this alternate space, the writer is freed to play with language while tracing its contours from a fresh perspective. Such an exceptional opportunity, however, came with arrival of war in Ukraine and by the reasons for its appearance there. Shaken by the upending of one's home, the author surrenders himself and his craft to an experiment with identity that has disturbing consequences. A result of this investigation is a novel that grants its readers inside access to a lively display of the ways that memory and language interplay in the construction of one's self. The novel lays bare the disruption and damage that come with displacement but also points towards a new sense of awareness that it can reveal.

Mondegreen is the seventh novel by Volodymyr Rafeyenko (b. 1969), but it is the first novel that he has written in the Ukrainian language. Prior to this novel, Rafeyenko had established himself as a successful Ukrainian Russophone writer. For the novel *Brief Farewell Book* (*Kratkaia kniga proshchanii*, 1999), he was awarded the Volodymyr Korolenko Prize of the National Writers' Union of Ukraine for the best Ukrainian prose written in Russian. His novel *The Length of Days* (*Dolgota dnei*, 2017), which was translated from Russian into Ukrainian by Marianna Kiyanovska, made the long list for the Shevchenko National Prize in 2018. That same year, the novel received the Visegrad Eastern Partnership Literary Award.[1]

Several of his novels have made the long and short lists of the Russian Prize, given to Russian-language writers living outside of Russia, including *Irrevocable Verbs* (*Nevozvratnye glagoly*, 2009), *All Through the Summer* (*Leto naprolet*, 2012), and *The Moscow Divertissement* (*Moskovskii divertisment*, 2011). His subsequent novel *Descartes' Demon* (*Demon Dekarta*, 2014) was awarded the Russian Prize and was finalist for the 2014 NOS Literature Prize.

Born, raised, and educated in Donetsk, the largest city in Ukraine's eastern-most Donbas region, Rafeyenko is a writer, a poet, a translator, a literary critic, an editor, and a film critic. He is also a scholar, who completed postgraduate studies in literary theory at Donetsk University. Additionally, he is the author of almost one hundred crime-fiction novels and popular-educational books written under a pseudonym.

***

The Revolution of Dignity (commonly known as the Maidan) arose in Ukraine in 2013–14, dramatically affecting the country's political landscape. In the autumn of 2013, after having indicated that he was charting Ukraine's vector West, towards Europe, the country's President, Viktor Yanukovych, abruptly adjusted Ukraine's future developments along Russian lines. Many Ukrainians took to the streets to express their displeasure, filling Independence Square (Maidan Nezalezhnosti) in its capital city of Kyiv and protesting in cities and towns around the country. After months of peaceful protests calling for an end to systemic corruption in the country, tensions rose in February 2014 and a violent crackdown by the Yanukovych regime ensued, propelling the revolution forward and ultimately resulting in the Ukrainian president's fleeing to Russia. At the beginning of March, a week after the Olympic Games had wrapped up in the Russian city of Sochi, Ukraine's Crimea was seized by Russia during a so-called referendum that was administered with the accompaniment of the Russian army. Pro-Russian protests in Ukraine's eastern and southern regions were supplemented by troops and commanders arriving from Russia. Eventually, two separatist regions were carved out in Ukraine's Donbas region and a war between Ukraine and Russia-backed rebels began.[2] As of the writing of this introduction in spring 2021, the war between Russia and Ukraine continues and has resulted in over 13,000 deaths. It has also led to the displacement of over one and half million people from Crimea and

from the occupied regions. One such refugee is Volodymyr Rafeyenko.

On July 12, 2014—one week after pro-Russian rebels
took over his native city of Donetsk—Rafeyenko left behind his life in the city and set off for Kyiv with $200 in
his pocket and two suitcases full of clothes.[3] He first ad-
dressed the topic of this war in his novel *The Length of the
Days*. Written in Russian, like all of his previous works,
the novel is an account of an invasion of Ukraine presented with elements of the grotesque and fantasy.[4] But
with *Mondegreen*, Rafeyenko took a more radical step in
approaching the war with his writing. Appalled that Russia had justified its invasion of Ukraine with the fabri-
cated excuse that they came to protect Russian-speaking
citizens of Ukraine from a nationalist Ukrainian "junta,"
Rafeyenko, as someone who spoke Russian and made
a living working in the Russian language while living
in Ukraine, felt like he was simultaneously a victim of
the war and, in some manner, responsible for it.[5] This
compelled him to not only flee his home town but to also
make a concerted effort to learn the Ukrainian language.
In Kyiv, where he now gives lectures on hermeneutics and
on the philosophy of art, and leads a unique workshop
for aspiring writers, Rafeyenko became acquainted with
Ukrainian-speaking writers and other artists and had
the opportunity to practice the language—an opportunity hard to come by in Donetsk. He had always enter-
tained the idea of someday attempting to write a novel
in Ukrainian and so decided that his next novel had to
be written in the language.[6] In fact, that novel, which
became *Mondegreen*, would largely be about its chief protagonist's interaction with the Ukrainian language.

***

Mondegreen: Songs about Death and Love was published in 2019 by the Meridian Czernowitz Publishing House, which regularly publishes the leading figures of contemporary Ukrainian literature, including Yuri Andrukhovych, Oksana Zabuzhko, and Serhiy Zhadan. The novel's appearance in one of Ukraine's most prestigious publishing houses was followed by its making the short list for the 2021 Shevchenko National Prize. It is Rafeyenko's first novel to be translated into English. The novel is the story of Haba Habriel Habinsky, a refugee who moves to Kyiv to escape a war that has transformed his native city Z (aka City Zero, a favorite sign of Rafeyenko's for war-ravaged Donetsk). Its plot mostly alternates between Haba's new life in Kyiv and his earlier life in city Z, but also includes scenes set in the Donbas a century earlier, as the Bolsheviks were establishing their control in Ukrainian lands.

Haba was a lecturer at the university in city Z but now has difficulty finding work as an intellectual in Kyiv. He ends up getting a job stocking shelves in a fancy supermarket located at a giant new shopping and entertainment complex typical of those that have appeared in Ukrainian cities in the 21st century. Haba also struggles to find friends in Kyiv and ends up socializing mostly with his boss at the supermarket, Petsia Petrovych Petrov, and his neighbor Lionia. This, in turn, leads to a rendezvous and the development of a relationship with Ole-Luk-Oie with whom he is able to explore the breadth of the Ukrainian language. Lacking the opportunity to learn the language in his Russified, native Donbas, Haba makes learning the language a priority after fleeing

Russian aggression there and moving to Ukraine's relatively less-Russified capital. As he sets off exploring an unknown, frenzied city, with its deep and vast Metro system, nouveau riche playthings, and plethora of ancient architectural monuments, in his new life, Haba is often visited by the Mare's Head, a frightening character from a Ukrainian folk tale (one of several to appear in the novel). The Mare's Head, visible only to Haba, intrudes on his budding romantic life and hijacks his study of Ukrainian. Haba's life is also disturbed by news of the murders in Kyiv of several refugees, who like he, had moved to the capital from the Donbas.

The passages about Haba's life in city Z flashback to scenes of Haba's puberty and mostly concern his love affair, as a university lecturer, with the diminutive student Sosipatra. Stories of intellectual and sexual life in city Z unfold alongside a depiction of its increasingly militarized atmosphere as the city transforms into a zone of aggression and its inhabitants into strange, incompatible partners. The Donbas of an earlier time also acts as a setting in the novel, a period in which Haba's ancestors clashed with forced collectivization in 1922 Soviet Ukraine. Stories of his family's struggles with trauma and survival reach Haba, offering potential avenues of guidance as he navigates the convoluted and perilous path treaded by a person displaced by war in his native land.

Displacement is just one of several key themes that Rafeyenko has opened the door to the exploration of in *Mondegreen*. The novel also offers the opportunity to examine the role of memory in the creation of identity and the particular role that language can play in its

development. *Mondegreen* focuses on change and transformation, scrutinizing the relationship between the
past and the present. The author is able to investigate
these topics by subjecting his chief protagonist Haba to
an existence where the line between reality and the imagined is as murky as are, sadly, present-day projections on
the future of Ukraine's Donbas region. Haba attempts
to traverse these two realms with the help of existing
philosophical and cultural frameworks, both eastern
and western—or, at least, distorted projections of these
systems.

Emotionally distraught from disorientation, loneli-
ness, and a shrouded, mutual mistrust between him and
those who now surround him, the displaced Haba experiences great difficulty in grabbing hold of his bearings in
his new life. And, having made the difficult, momentous
choice to leave behind his friends and family in city Z,
Haba undergoes a deep reevaluation of his established
personal convictions. The chief object of his investigation
becomes that which he remembers as his past. In his novel, Rafeyenko alludes to the subjectivity and constructed
nature of one's memories. Utilizing a metaphor of an ed-
ited movie, he exposes the selectivity that is engaged in
creating memory.

Transformation is another major theme of *Mondegreen*, and the novel is dotted with scenes of nature, people, and cities—all in a state of change. This underlying
topic of alteration in the novel leads to questions about
how change affects one's identity. If identity is capable
of change, then what does that change do to the past,
to memory, to long-held interpretations of the world?

What then happens to that former self? Does it disappear? Is it now irrelevant?

Haba's self undergoes a deep transformation as a result of his displacement, and this shift is confounded by his choice to adopt a new language. In *Mondegreen* we see how language itself affects memory. Haba's decision to learn the Ukrainian language throws the protagonist into disarray. The new language repositions his relations to things and people. The novel plays extensively with the idea of naming. Rafeyenko tinkers with the multiple meanings of words—the same word can have two different meanings, while two different words can have the same meaning. Most of *Mondegreen*'s protagonists have several names, or variations of their names, which Rafeyenko constantly revolves, including that of its chief protagonist, Haba. This feature hints at the existence of multiple, complex memories within one person and in fluid identities—characteristics that are not foreign in today's Ukraine.

The multiple names and meanings, and the similarly sounding names, that pervade *Mondegreen* are consistent with the novel's title and its exploration of subjectivity. A mondegreen is something that is heard incorrectly, something that is understood by a person to be something it is not. As such, the meaning of something is based on how one hears it, how one interprets it, and how it has been filtered through one's experiences. And although it may be a false meaning, that person considers it to be the proper meaning. It also calls to mind how misnaming can lead to misunderstanding between people. The novel's enhanced focus on language constantly brings to the fore the ways that different languages feature different words for the same object and how that can change shades of their meaning. These explorations of language that are able to take place because the novel's chief protagonist is shown to be in the process of learning a language are given additional depth as its author is simultaneously subjecting himself to the very same process. By boldly having chosen to write *Mondegreen* in Ukrainian, Rafeyenko is able to add another layer to his investigation of language and identity.

The disorder that Haba is subjected to because of these various substantial changes to his life leave him in a damaged mental and emotional state. Throughout the novel it is difficult to determine whether what Haba is seeing and doing is actually taking place or only taking place in his mind. The line between illusion and reality is constantly being crossed in this novel. There is much that is opaque in *Mondegreen* with its unexpected allusions and its many fantastic scenes—they are consistent with the psychological malady that Haba undergoes on its pages. However, this constant state of living in both reality and imagination also suggests the possibility that Haba, in straddling these two worlds, can act as an intermediary between them. His name, Habriel (Ukrainian for Gabriel), hints at his being like the Angel Gabriel—someone capable of connecting two different realms. Haba is able to do this because of his recent painful experiences and due to the changes he is undergoing. And although all these changes have led Haba to this damaged state, they have also connected him to a repressed past that is an essential component of his, and his nation's, identity.

Mondegreen is a novel replete with references to cultural, religious, and scientific figures and systems. Christian scripture appears on the novel's first pages and religion continues to be turned to throughout the book. References to the Greek-Egyptian god Hermes Trismegistus, the Chinese philosopher Zhuang Zhou, and Marcel Proust's protagonist Swann are just some of the calls for help made by Haba in the novel in what are attempts to get hold of his fleeting memory. Other references, including numerous quotes of Ukrainian and Russian poetry and popular songs, and even the Beatles, serve to add commentary to the narrative and, often, to humorously color a generally dense text. All of these references act as part of Haba's search for some type of stability among the chaos that has engulfed him.

Perhaps the key direct reference that is made in the novel is the one made to the Mare's Head. There are several variations of Ukrainian folk tales featuring the Mare's Head. Most involve an old man and woman, their daughters, and the frightening skull of a mare's head—all setting the scene for a test of morals. It is the varying interactions of the daughters with the Mare's Head that determine the girls' different fates. The Mare's Head, the skull of a dead mare, symbolizes deceased relatives. And respect for one's ancestors leads to life and prosperity while disrespect leads to decay and death. In *Mondegreen*, it is Haba's eventual acknowledgement of the story of his great-grandparents that opens up a path to his potential healing.

***

A novel with such a concentrated text and so full of hidden allusions certainly brings many challenges to the

translator. Additionally, of course, passing along historical and cultural contexts from the source language to
the language of the target audience brings further dif-
ficulties. Thus, in translating the novel for the English-
language reader, I decided to footnote references that
would most likely be known to the Ukrainian-language
reader but not necessarily to the reader of this translation. I also provided notes on a few, but not all, of the
myriad references Rafeyenko makes in his novel, choosing to elucidate those that I deemed be the most crucial
to fully appreciating the novel. As I have written above,
Mondegreen is a novel that is very much about language.
Its author scatters language games throughout the
text, which help keep the novel's complex narrative and
weighty subject matter flowing remarkably smooth-
ly while also sustaining the book's focus on language.
Where possible, I tried to render his linguistic play into
English but, in some cases, I needed to provide notes to
explain some of the nuances that could not be passed
along in translation.

The fact that both the author of *Mondegreen* and its
chief protagonist are, in essence, learning the language
as the novel unfolds leads to several instances where
Rafeyenko clearly exhibits his joy in crafting with a new
language, with all of its strange beauty, nuances, and
peculiarities. This is evident, for example, when the author (and Haba) utilizes the vocative case. Used when
addressing someone or something, the vocative case
does not exist in the Russian language, and takes on
a certain joyful, exotic quality for a "first-time user" in
the novel. Similarly, the author seems to relish in the use
of the extensive arsenal of diminutives that are found

in the Ukrainian language. Perhaps reflecting both the author and protagonist gradually getting a hold of the Ukrainian language as the novel progresses, the first few pages of the novel feature a viscous collage of Ukrainian and English-language names, many Russian words and phrases, and Old Church Slavonic. And there are also comparisons made between Russian and Ukrainian words and, in one case, an intentionally-poor Ukrainian translation of a popular Russian song.

The distance one sometimes experiences when hearing, reading, speaking, or writing in a learned, yet non-native, language, can certainly interfere with fully grasping that language. However, it also creates an opportunity for that person to see and hear that language from a perspective that a native speaker does not have. This can be beneficial when playing with the language and this phenomenon is certainly experienced when reading Rafeyenko's Ukrainian text. And, for someone who also experiences a distance from Ukrainian, I tried to keep that phenomenon in mind when translating the text.

Of course, in some instances, things simply could not be passed along in translation. My hope is that they are few and do not detract from enjoying this novel as it was written. As always, I thank my wife Yaryna Yakubyak, with whom I consulted while untangling many of the linguistic intricacies and references made in the novel. I am also grateful to Polina Peker for helping me to share with her father certain questions I had while I was working on the translation of his novel.

***

Mondegreen: Songs about Death and Love is a prime example of the profound ways that Ukrainian culture has been stimulated by the Russian-Ukrainian war in the Donbas. Ukrainian artists have responded to the disruption and horrors of the war by producing diverse, probing, and innovative works of literature, visual art, music, and film. The topics of memory, gender, and identity, that have invigorated post-Soviet Ukrainian literature for the past three decades are approached in an original manner, providing refreshed perspectives to these crucial issues. As the war endures, this "culture of war" itself develops along novel technologies and in new forms. It has already been the subject of scholarly analysis and will undoubtedly continue to be so.[7] Gradually, access to these cultural breakthroughs for people outside of Ukraine has grown.[8] In the field of literature, besides this publication, published English-language translations of Ukrainian literary works that feature the topic of the Russian-Ukrainian war on its pages include: *Letters from Ukraine: Poetry Anthology*, comp. Hryhory Semenchuk (Kolo, 2016); *Words for War: New Poems from Ukraine*, ed. Oksana Maksymchuk & Max Rosochinsky (Academic Studies Press, 2017); Natalya Vorozhbit, *Bad Roads*, trans. by Sasha Dugdale (Nick Hern Books, 2017); *The White Chalk of Days: The Contemporary Ukrainian Literature Series Anthology*, ed. Mark Andryczyk (Academic Studies Press, 2017); *The Frontier: 28 Contemporary Ukrainian Poets—An Anthology*, ed. Anatoly Kudryavitsky (Glagoslav, 2017); Yuri Andrukhovych, *My Final Territory: Selected Essays*, trans. by Mark Andryczyk and Michael M. Naydan (University of Toronto Press, 2018);

Serhiy Zhadan, *What to Live for, What to Die for: Selected Poems*, trans. by Virlana Tkacz and Wanda Phipps (Yale University Press, 2019); Oleg Sentsov, *Life Went on Anyway: Stories*, trans. by Uilleam Blacker (Deep Vellum, 2019); Artem Chekh, *Absolute Zero*, trans. by Olena Jennings and Oksana Lutsyshyna (Glagoslav, 2020); Serhiy Zhadan, *A New Orthography*, trans. by John Hennessy and Ostap Kin (Lost Horse Press, 2020); Serhiy Zhadan, *The Orphanage*, trans. by Reilly Costigan-Humes and Isaac Stackhouse Wheeler (Yale University Press, 2021); Lyuba Yakimchuk, *Apricots of Donbass*, trans. by Oksana Maksymchuk, Max Rosochinsky, and Svetlana Lavochkina (Lost Horse Press, 2021); and Stanislav Aseyev, *In Isolation: Dispatches from Occupied Donbas* (Ukrainian Research Institute, Harvard University, 2022).

***

Mondegreen's first and last sentences include allusions to Ukrainian Christmas carols (in Ukrainian, *koliady*). *Koliady* bring to mind scenes of loved ones gathering to celebrate traditions that have been passed along through families for centuries. Like *koliady*, Ukrainian folk tales are consistently repeated as they are told from generation to generation. These tales often feature fantastic stories with unnerving plots, that somehow (may) become comforting with repetition. Rafeyenko explores very difficult, universal subjects in his novel *Mondegreen*—subjects that have been dramatically highlighted by the intrusion of war in his homeland. The author has chosen to explore these issues in a correspondingly complex literary work full of fragments of songs, poems, and folk tales, and

featuring an intricate plot that weaves through attempt-
ed recreations of past reality. Through this complexity,
however, two things become apparent after reading the
novel: that what is important is not just the stories that
you have been told, but also those that you have not; and
that the novel's main story is not so much about escaping
as it is about returning.

Who are you, Lord?
   —Saul

The mare's head knocked-n-rocked.
   —"The Mare's Head"

Not so young, sir, to love a woman for singing, nor
so old to dote on her for anything. I have years
on my back forty-eight.
   —William Shakespeare, *King Lear*

On Essence

I looked at all the little lambs —
Those are not my little lambs!
I looked back at the village huts —
I don't have a village hut!
    —Taras Shevchenko

What could be the essence of all of this, O master? Haba breathed in the frigid Kyiv air and pondered how this year's autumn had been so warm and yet the cold came so quickly, seemingly out of nowhere, and how this was a real mind-fuck. Well what then could be the essence of all of this? And what is the Ukrainian essence, if you compare it with, say, the Russian one? Of course, the Ukrainian essence, if it is our national one, should be different from the essential essence, so to say, of the enemy? Right? Or are there certain philosophical coordinates where the national disappears and the essentially human sets out upon its difficult and senseless path? Can we suppose that Russians are inhuman? That Ukrainians, for example, are humans while Russians are—the reverse (*the re-verse—what a wonderful word; re-creation? A time of reproduction? And Jesus said to them, "Truly, I say to you, when the Son of Man will sit on his glorious throne, you who have followed me in the re-creation will also sit on twelve thrones, judging the twelve tribes of Israel*).[1] And if we are to accept this, well then how about the French or, more generally, the Europeans? How do you co-exist with them? All those Sartres, Camus, and Levis—what are they, biologically speaking? Deleuze, Derrida, Barthes. And Darwin in particular (*Charles Robert Darwin*)? And where the hell did this curious theologian come from? And couldn't some virtuous person have showed up and bashed his bones with a baseball bat to stop him from writing that idiocy of his about people and monkeys having common relatives? Well tell me this, Mr. Theologian. Do you get a kick out of a monkey and wise men having common relatives?

Of course not, it's all very clear. Homo sapiens—or, as it is proper to say now, Homo sapiens sapiens—with all your sadness and intoxication, well, who haven't you slept with, you loser, especially in those knotty 1990s. And what then can be said about the 2000s and 2010s, which were filled to the rim with fire.

You know, sometimes things line up in such a way that it becomes unbearable. The soul gets torn by a sense that life is expiring and pulling away from you, like the nighttime local train to Publiieve-Neronove (*the same as Klavdiieve-Tarasove, a small town in the Borodiansk district of Kyiv oblast. Founded in 1903, located 1,440.71 miles from Paris. At the fork, stay to the right and continue on A4/E25/E50; follow the signs toward Paris/Luxembourg/Thionville*), which flickers its phantom fires. And, moreover, a spiritual development doesn't come at all. You look back into past days and they are empty, and instead of a greater awareness ringing in the radiance of a fullness of existence, you are left with the bland, concrete slice of cake of a provincial railway platform. Empty packs of cigarettes, sunflower seed shells, a half-empty bottle of Chernihiv Light beer, a homeless dude on a bench reading Conan Doyle. The wind spreads yellow dust. And, standing up to your ears in that dust, you come to understand that you haven't done anything worthy in your life (*existence is bleeding to death, looking into you with the sad eyes of dead relatives and folk tale characters*).

And it is in that state that sapiens sapiens drifts through the woods. In that state. And there's a monkey sleeping there. Can you believe it, dear compatriots? This guy is preoccupied with existence, while the monkey just fucking sleeps. This guy's sadness has got him by the balls, while the monkey, drunk off champagne, lies beneath the walnut tree. The bodhisattvas of Ukraine. Each in its own manner, of course. And that is where relatives come from.

It would be better for this Darwin to ask whom his mother slept with. This theologian. Why is he picking on monkeys? There are so many animals in our society that that spiel about monkeys—it's not even half the truth. It's only a quarter of the problem. I wonder why he didn't write anything about those wild boars, crows, hedgehogs, rats, butterflies, dragonflies, dogs and wolves, bears, snakes, laughing and crying hyenas, and just a few innocent woodpeckers, that make up our political scene? It's a real frog-fest, this parliament.

"But why is it Darwin that I am attacking?" Haba suddenly wondered.

Why not Martin Luther? And the fact that he's German doesn't mean anything. Germans, actually, are the same way, except that they are fonder of order. If you should break some sort of law, like, for example, deciding to take a leak in the middle of the Brandenburg Gate, then your friend-bursche, with whom you had just been downing beers in a bar, will turn you in to the police, you can be sure of that. Even if you were a proponent of, say, anarcho-radicalism.

"So then, what is all this leading to?"

Well, who knows, master, what this is all leading to, Haba shrugged his shoulders, but I am learning a language. A language so musical and magical. One that leads you to all kinds of nonsense and multicolored idiocy, it calls you to March madness, to holy hollow November. You can mumble non-stop about anything in this language for a hundred thousand years, and speak gobbledygook with your tangled, refugee tongue. (*Gobelen? Gusk? Let's home in on that rabbit and his balls*).

And it is at this moment that Haba thought that, perhaps, he is beginning to develop a polyglot syndrome. While talking to himself only in his native Russian, he remained an average Joe. But when he began learning a second language, all sorts of God-knows-what began entering his brain. From much knowledge, there is much despair.

"That is the fate of today's intellectuals," he said to himself, sighed heavily, and, with a dawdling sadness, breathed the lively air of perpetual expulsion into his greying beard, made the sign of the cross, and continued strolling down Obolon Avenue.

Well, what the heck can you do, it's autumn. Autumn. And what is autumn? It is the onset of a turning point. The sky cries in blood beneath your feet. And stupid crows scuttle through the puddles. Kyivan crows, fucking eh.[2]

"So then," Haba mumbled, "why the hell didn't you, Mr. Pushkin, tell us anything? You were a pretty decent chap. And talented. If you saw a Jew, you would say to him: look at the Jew. If you saw a babe, then you'd say: ababahalamaha.[3] And then you'd grab her by her skirt. Come here, sugar. He brought her to his corner, wrung his hands, sat her tied-up on a stool and said to her in perfect German: I am your Sacher-Masoch, mein daaarling. I brought you to the City of the Lion itself. I'll start telling your tales, calling you *pannochka*, you'll be a sexually satisfied chick. You'll become a true *halychanka*.[4] But she says to him: go fuck yourself, you perverted horse, damn you! I ain't no *halychanka*, I'm the French novelist and playwright Honoré de Balzac. The novel sequence *La Comédie humaine*, which presents a panorama of post-Napoleonic French life, is generally viewed as my magnum opus. And I have such long, curly hair, because I curl it on giant nails forged in a metallurgic guild, and that's how I sleep, after drinking Marsala and smoking weed. I wake up in the morning looking flawlessly beautiful. And I could share this good fortune with you.

***

Haba entered the subway station and placed his card up against the square of unfathomable supply. It immediately replied that, apparently, he was free to enter. But it also informed him that Haba could only have access to Kyiv's innards three more times. An average refugee's entrance to a metro station is very strictly regulated.

Haba slowly slid down the stairs. In the horrific depths of the underground, glowing in a ghastly electricity that is carried by the winds from nearby hell, trains run along waves in demonic ventilators of human souls. There's always just a scattering of people here in the evenings. Everyone is heading somewhere. The old, the young, the Russian-speakers, the Ukrainian-speakers. Tatars, the French, Jews, the English, the Chinese, the Vietnamese, Russians, Roma, Romanians, Moldovans. Girls and boys. The readers of Andrii Kokotiukha[5] and of Augustine Aloysius Joyce. Fans of innovative sex and of conventional sex. A whole Babylon is shifting somewhere underground, and this mixing of human streams is senseless. It is clear that the city of Kyiv is insane. For it's the city of the mother of Rus´ and an elderly and somewhat cataleptic one at that.[6] And this is felt. And the Kyiv metro is the quintessence of this. If, of course, the Ukrainian language has the word "quintessence."

And Haba was unsure about that fact and so he saddened, sensing how the Kyiv autumn tumbled down here to him from the surface above. Like that stubborn mare's head. In an attempt to cheer himself up a bit he once again began to mumble a few, in essence primitive, in essence extremely banal, energetically sentimental lines about autumn.

Autumn. Boats are burnt down to the ground. Hey-hey-hey-without a sound. Hey-hey-hey, nothin' but hey-hey-hey.[7] Just when you start translating something truly energetic and sentimental, the translating bug abandons you and you are left standing naked and in shambles (*by the way the root "sham" (sic!) comes from the traditional Japanese musical instrument—the shamisen, which itself is derived from a Chinese instrument, a refugee of sorts*) smack in the center of culture, like a pink monkey on a stage. An altogether unpleasant feeling.

Haba looked at the mob that packed into the train together with him but then found a map and settled down. Mr. Pushkin said nothing. That's for sure. But, gentlemen, if you're going to blame someone then it should be Nestor the Chronicler. And, actually, a whole bunch of wonderful people before him. Let's say, John the Evangelist. I mean, come on, man, if you indeed saw those four horsemen in your dreams, those that flew in to bomb Syria, then why didn't you write just that? As in, dear people, what can I tell you about Armageddon. You read my Apocalypse, or should I say αποκαλυψις (*the train isn't going any farther, the stop is Heroïv Dnipra, cream, icy-cream, lima bean, protein, sea bream, sunshine on my shoulder makes me happy, mama ooh-ooh-ooh*).

Suddenly, Haba noticed that, one, he had fallen asleep for a few minutes and, two, for those few minutes he was once again heading in the wrong direction. Fatigue, like an insidious and hard-working woman, never stops cultivating your brain. Haba yawned, glanced at the backs of the final passengers and exited the train. He stood for a few seconds, sensing how the recent five-minute blackout had changed something in him, jerked his shoulders (*a certain wicked force jerked his entire stiff body, bent him over, twisted his bruised bones in pain*) and went over to the opposite side of the platform.

So what's this all about? Ok. Here it is. Mr. Jonah. "The Apocalypse," of course, is approached here solely metaphorically, perhaps—in a postmodern manner, maybe somewhat surrealistically or biblically-symbolically. As if viewed from an ivory tower. But he could have also stated it honestly, not taking into account the centuries of future (*past*) space, and cut to the chase: you, Ukrainians, know that when the Russian Khaganate begins bombarding Mesopotamia—worldwide doom looms near you. And not—past those forests, and not—past those trees, but here, by the "barbacan" and the "cupidon."[8]

Once again, he traveled beneath the ground, glancing occasionally at the map in the dark window beyond which he imagined an endless obscurity of long, damp tunnels, filled with traces left behind by people for eternity. Pictures, inspirations, faces, thoughts, life and sadness, the warm, brazen, and nonetheless not-yet-final death of sapiens sapiens, fated to remain forevermore within this hoard, within these walls, in this echo that gaits in the metro's underground since the beginning of time. At a certain point, the current era fades away, doors are closing, the next stop—eternity, and shadows continue to traverse between the walls of the tunnel until morning. The shadows of forgotten ancestors.[9] They think that they are people, that someone awaits them at the other end of their hopeless journey.

The metro absorbs everything that's human, accumulates it, and transforms it into the beyond. Three minutes in this train and a person no longer belongs to oneself, will never see oneself, although, of course, will also never forget oneself. Seconds will pass, they'll add up to minutes and hours, you'll go up to your reflection in a pool of water and say to it: I am your child. The water ripples and replies: You're no child, you're just a regular brat, a simple reflection, bro.

In other words, every ass knows: whether you choose to follow the map or not, the paths that subway trains travel are not dependent on it. And generally, neither does your life. This, of course, is silly—constantly staring at the red, green, and blue lines of the metro map. This is lunacy. Even if your suspicions are justified, and these lines—like everything else in this beautiful city—change into their opposites every minute (*"betrayal-victory," a purely Ukrainian form of the "body-soul" dualism*), there's nothing you can do about it. So, forget about it, buddy, forget about all this crap, don't follow the lines on that imagined map, it's just as much of a ghost as is, by the way, everyone near you. There is no one. You are alone in this city—nobody needs that stupid sliver of light, that microscopic bit of warmth, that grey mind, those black eyes, those yellow Easter eggs, that never satisfied staff of love, that liver that craves Borjomi mineral water, that sun—a red little star glowing somewhere in the chest, that stunning and insidious thing known as the "I." Actually, that last thing is also absent, although it is still entitled to a whole three rides on this metro.

But no matter what Haba would say to himself, no matter how he tried to convince himself, he would always become unsettled if he couldn't see the metro map. What a provincial chump.

***

Haba wound up in this city not too long ago. Approximately X number of years ago, at the beginning of a certain century. It doesn't matter exactly when he left his occupied home. He grabbed his rags and moved to the city of the sacral Ukr-force. Many good things awaited him here. For example, the absence of the Islamic State, of the Ebola virus and of Russian tourists.[10] But many surprises also emerged in everyday life. They jumped up from non-existence like a Jack in the Box and required attention. There were both pleasant and unpleasant surprises. There were those that, at the outset, would elicit neither positive nor negative energy but would nonetheless suck up a great deal of the refugee's spiritual health. Like, let's say, the metro, or the Obolon women.

But the most overwhelming revelation was the Ukrainian language. It was melodious and delightful. On the one hand, this was the language that was spoken to little Haba in his childhood days by the nightingale, the mouse, the rooster, and the wonderful worm. Let alone the mare's head. On the other hand, the fact of the matter was that he now had to converse with it, that worm, regularly.

How can this be explained? It is difficult but what can you do.

So, here's the deal. Haba read in Ukrainian almost since he was a kid. He liked reading in Ukrainian, although it was much easier to read in Russian. And he wasn't able to speak in Ukrainian at all. Because there was no one in his hometown with whom he could speak in that language. As an adult, he befriended a couple of smart and respectable Ukrainian-speaking guys, but they only spoke Ukrainian amongst themselves, perhaps, preserving in that manner a dedication to the Ukrainianophile guild. Several times Haba asked them to speak to

him in Ukrainian, to accept him into their circle of clandestine and nationally-conscious individuals. And he, of
course, promised not to tell anyone about this and that he
would take this secret with him to the grave (*only patriots
would speak Ukrainian in the Donbas and the Ukrainian intel-
ligentsia from beyond the Dnipro River almost never came here*).
Those wonderful molfars[11] of the Donbas would smile
about this. They were evasive, they cordially expressed
their shame. But when they would pick up some vodka
and snacks and sit around a table they would nonetheless
switch to Russian. It was easier for them that way.

Haba understood this phenomenon. Assimilation was
a completely reasonable desire in a city where, stretching
back to Paleolithic times, the locals would ask Putin to
bring his army (*crazed mammoths circle around, pro-Russian
placards flutter by the regional administrative building*).

But the conduct of these guys was somewhat different. For example, they truly loved their language. But
deep in their souls they believed that there was no sense
conversing with inhabitants of the Donbas in this language. It was like casting pearls before swine. Ok, *excu-
sez-moi*, maybe not so categorically—maybe not before
swine but before, let's say, hedgehogs, little worms, or
cute squirrels. Before clumsy and deficient beavers and
raccoons. But what the hell is the difference? These guys
were ashamed of their language, and they were ashamed
of themselves before this language. Both inferiority and
a great, genuine Irish pride simmered in the compote
of their startlingly-provincial consciousness and there
was nothing you that could be done. That is why, kiddos,
Ukraine had no chances for finding mutual understanding between the various layers of the intellectual elite and

for the formation of a unified nation of pork-fat eaters and Russki-haters. No one was interested in establishing a common cultural space. Not to mention space travel or smart, fair, individual language quotas. At least not within the Donbas. But hold on—our Ukraine is the one and only—not a country, but a doll! (*The teacher looks ponderingly at the class. The class (ponderingly)—at the teacher. A holiness glows from the students. Hallelujah, the children say in a choir. The school rises to the heavens and disappears among the clouds.*)

So then. Obviously, there was no sense in uttering something to oneself in Ukrainian. They could have sent you to the nuthouse for that. And then there would be no way back for Haba. So, what sense was there in conversing? None. Language needs to be living and vital. It's the one that needs this—not us.

The final kiss from the woman of your dreams, the travels of Marco Polo, a liturgy in a village church, where the only ones present are you and an old priest, the Mother of God in St. Cyril's Church, angels painted by Vrubel, using psych-ward patients as models[12] (*Pavlovsk Psychoneurologic Hospital No. 1, those angels live there to this day*), a mug of hemlock offered to you by a pleasant person, talking for hours with deceased friends, and, first and foremost—a future love that reveals itself in the most fragile of premonitions—all of this is language. Something that is born from language, is sustained by language, and becomes language. Language is many things. But it must be needed. Because then you use it and it forms you. This mechanism works like the Eucharist. You receive its body, wash it down with cold raisin-flavored *kvas*, and fly through the heavens from morning 'til night.

At any rate, that which Haba had accepted calmly before the war had become increasingly uncomfortable once it began. Not speaking the official language of Ukraine, especially while living in its capital, Kyiv, in a time of war *just ain't right*. If you know what I mean.

When Habinsky arrived in Kyiv, he observed that, for the most part, the city speaks the same wonderful language that the enemy does, just with more mistakes. The junta[13] considered itself to be a Ukrainian one, but the language that predominated in the city was Russian. Schrödinger's famous cat paradox, in fact, dictates that Ukraine exists but you can't see it. It's both dead and alive, like our mother nature, or, in fact, Ukrainian statehood.

But Haba was not flummoxed, and stuck to his plan. He studied Ukrainian on his own. And, to speed up the process, at some point he began talking to himself exclusively in Ukrainian. Because, he would ask himself, from where would authentic Ukrainian culture come to Kyiv if not from Donetsk?

What is this insanity, you may ask, how can something good come out of Nazareth? That is, in a purely genetic, and thus, scholarly-national, sense. In this Galilea, dear ladies and gentlemen, you've got pagans and coalminers. There, blood is so uncertainly and variably mixed with coal and with the grey clouds of the steppe that there can be no genetic hope for something groovy. Because genetics and vegetarianism, as everyone knows, are *everything* to us. Or perhaps not *everything*?

Phillip will smile, check the level of oxygen in the coalmine and say: "Come and you'll see with your own eyes, my dears, come and you'll see!" And maybe someday you will dare to do so, but not now—no, not now, by any means.

While still riding in *Passenger Train Donetsk-Z—Mother-Kyiv*, Haba Habinsky decided to do everything possible and impossible to grasp that musical language, even if it were to take him a few years. At least at the level of Maeterlinck or, let's say, Herbert Wells. And why not? But it turned out that, regarding language, who actually grasps whom is not so clear.

***

In life, beginning with the day we are born, we are continuously subject to surprises. They can also be called the unexpecteds or the undesireds. These may sound a bit admixed but what can you do. So then, after two-three months of diligent study, it turned out that trying to learn the Ukrainian language, for an adult who has chosen to resettle, is mentally dangerous. The honest efforts of an individual who completely and fully desires to resettle (and not only in the geographical sense), to settle in a place (*to set, to set up house, to make a settlement, to settle for, to settle up, to settle down, to settle on a place*), and the young age associated with that language meet and transform into characters from folk stories and into various mythological figures, giving birth to ruinous protuberances of memory. And this, my friends, is truly terrifying.

And before these characters appear, a person becomes frightened to tears by a new, horrific and incomprehensible, linguistic memory. One day it lands right inside your brain—*hello, my fluffy kitten*—after which the refugee cannot understand what it was that they had actually experienced in their life and what they by no means hadn't. Especially in Donetsk. Especially in the one that no longer exists and no longer will. And did it ever exist? Maybe not. And this is not a joke.

Through the memories of a non-existent past, through folk tales and dreams, the refugee, and even more so this rarified version of him—the refugee-polyglot—finally comes face to face with being. That which, following Parmenides, only is today, is never in the past, is never in the future. Language enters this polyglot completely, immovably, and excessively, like that concrete feeling of excitement[14] after good coitus, like May in February, like thoughts after death, or blue circles on dead water.

And only later, this excessiveness of language, of course, finds very concrete, although not always comfortable or understood, representations. For example, already in those very first months after he began studying the language, this neo-Kyivite began to receive rather regular visits from the mare's head (or the MR[15]). And although the worm, the nightingale, and the black and white rooster appeared much earlier, we must admit that this whole process, to put it mildly, did not improve the psychiatric state of this bilingual Ukrainian.

But we shouldn't complain. We needn't waste time on useless grief. Enough, as a certain poetess wrote, no more complaining, no more crying.[16] It's better to get to the point and talk about the mare's head. And, indeed, what is this phenomenon—this mare's head? Besides all of the complexities in the question itself, the initial approach to it is very simple. If you know the mare well, then you potentially know everything you need to know about the mare's head. You just have to imagine the gigantic head of a mare—only without the mare itself. That is, the head and the neck—an object with a diameter of about three-four yards. And on this head, draw proportionally sad eyes and a nose. Large yellow twisted teeth in the mare's mouth should be a bit thinned-out like steel bones in the mouth of a sperm whale. You'll say that there are no steel bones in the mouth of a sperm whale, but you'll be incorrect: there are. The MR has a beautiful black mane. And draw a WWI-era war hat on top of it. The kind that Josef Švejk wore in the times of the Austro-Hungarian Empire.

The mare's head is a familiar character for Haba. His grandma, whose Eastern *Surzhyk*-laden Ukrainian[17] was her native language, would tell him that folk tale about it countless times during the terrifying years of his childhood. Little Haba thought a lot about the MR when he turned three–four years old. And later, too, if you think about it, year after year, regardless of his maturation. Haba forgot neither the nightingale nor the insidious coalminer worm, who, in one of the tales (*as it was recalled now*) would seek out lazy kids at night and eat their ears.

Imagine a child dozing off in bed, looking at lampposts outside his window (*they flicker and quietly ring, like celestial spheres*) and at little stars, smiling at the pink kitten that eats *varenyky*[18] with snow-white sour cream on the blue moon (*in essence—Gogol, it's all Gogol's fault*) and listening to the wind. But when midnight arrives, after the final horn sounds at the metallurgical factory (*with its forlorn forging*) the kid's room becomes a headquarters for pain and unbelievable horror.

Not a boy's scream but a beastly, heavy howl fills the room. And the wind no longer sings but moans outside the window like a devil's snowstorm, a snowsquall, a blizzard, or a whiteout (*depends on which lexeme you fancy at this time*). Shadows fly and cry. A five-cornered antique mirror rattles within its own frame. No longer able to reflect reality, it has blackened and become covered with metal wrinkles.

The worm, with a long moustache (*usually named Laurentius*), in old-fashioned glasses and sorrowful blue eyes, and with a smoking cigarette held by tweezers, sits on a boy's chest and ponderingly gnaws the child's ears, periodically spitting out bright blood on the floor, inhales, and goes back to gnawing. Occasionally he bites. In that case, a bloody stream shoots out from the jugular into the ceiling. The crystal chandelier above the bed, all damp and pink, clinks, chinks, dings, and pings. A jangly beast. That ceiling lamp seemingly doesn't know what's going on. However, it is precisely from it that the cries of the little boy stem. A bloodied dad and mom don't know what to do, or how to act.

"It's your fault," the father yells, "You let him watch Soviet cartoons after 9PM when he should have been studying the Ukrainian alphabet."

"Damn you," the mother begs, shaking her fist, "Damn you, oh father, the child needs to be saved, we can argue later."

The father grabs a guitar hanging on the wall and quickly tunes it.

"One, two, three, four," he grunts out, ignoring the wails of his favorite offspring. "*Yesterday, all my troubles seemed so far away.*"

"*Now it looks as though they're here to stay,*" the mother chimes in.

"*Oh, I believe in yesterday,*" they try taking it slow. The mom cries and sings, the dad, white as a wall, holds the rhythm steady, and the guitar too. Yes, all these bad things have arrived, have come together, and only a belief in yesterday allows you to carry on.

The worm, hearing the first chords, stops sucking the boy's ears and listens attentively. He closes his eyes and smiles. The little boy stops wailing, sniffles for a few more minutes, and groans, but grows calmer as his parents continue singing. Starting with the second verse, a quiet, blue, minty, cool rain that pours right from the ceiling gradually washes away the traces of the horror that has passed. The worm yawns, falls asleep, disappears.

***

Of course, of all the ghosts of childhood, the only one that remains unforgettable is the MR. It is because of it, by the way, that Haba had always had trouble with women, from the beginning of his sex life and throughout his existence. He imagined that every woman had that folk tale creature within her and that it was just waiting for Haba to hesitate and lose his focus. And, as was usually the case, Haba would inevitably lose that focus like the last Lancelot, that is *Lancelot of the Lake*.[19] He would fall in love with a beautiful and insidious Guinevere at the most inappropriate times in his life. And he was not able to get out of those situations without undergoing major damage. They all had the signs of everyday frivolity, useless stupidity, wonderful inevitability, and truly uncorrectable results. Idiocy, vividness, and otherworldliness—those are three butterflies on which he would base his love for women.

A solid foundation, a firm bedrock. Like that MR that has been tumbling across Europe for centuries, stubbornly hunting for the ghost of communism.

But it cannot be said that the MR really scared Haba much during puberty. Nothing special took place in those years. Just a normal period. You flip through the pages of encyclopedias and anthologies, you study the features of Egyptian, Ancient Greek, and Mesopotamian culture. Do you remember all of those women, boy? All those beautiful nudes, a product of the creativity of notorious sapiens sapiens? There's a good amount of them in art atlases, in various anthologies, in all kinds of histories of painting. How did you like India when you were thirteen, buddy? The Baroque? The Renaissance? The portrayal of women in the art of Peter Paul Rubens—that's its own epoch. To a certain extent, the whole essence of puberty is personified in Rubens. Mounds of naked fat and meat are purportedly there to depict mythological scenes—that in fact is puberty in its purest form, not overshadowed with religious reflection.

Woman as a study of transformation—that point of view constantly accompanied Habinsky. During his school years, the everyday and anytime tension of this discourse interfered with living and breathing. Women represented unbelievable joy, insurmountable longing, and unobtainable happiness. He should have had them all, all the world's women, initially all at once, and then each one separately. The women of the past, present, and future. In love and in marriage. In long lasting relationships and beyond its borders. In passenger trains and subways, in the parks of Berlin and Vienna, Kyiv and Wroclaw. In quiet churches and loud hotels, in Lviv

trolleys and Swedish barges, in the Ukrainian Carpath-
ians and in the Italian Alps. In the current of anguish
and in the Jacuzzi of unbearable joy. He should have had
them. But he did not—unfortunately or fortunately. And
not, of course, in that sense and not because of those reasons which you are surely thinking about at this time.

If you need to know, in bed, when the time finally arrived, Haba turned out to be fabulous. Like a bream that
has been captured by its glistening libido. Like a rabbit,
brave, invincible, and unattainable in its love making.
And still today he is able to make love seven years in
a row non-stop with any woman who comes to him in his
dreams and in his imagination. And only in the morning
of the eighth year, he'll sheepishly smile a bit and ask for
a cup of coffee and a slice of cheese.

"Listen," he will say, "baby, can you make me a cup of
coffee?"

You, the playful sweetie, young and uncaptured for
centuries, will weakly smile at him, spread your arms
wide, begin romping about, playing, laughing, and tick-
ling him. (*All go to one place: all come from dust and to dust all
return. Eccl.*) And then you, supposedly not on purpose,
will touch the inside of his thighs with your long-since
returned to dust tongue (*all go to one place, remember this
for seven thousand years*). You'll maneuver it, beginning at
the knees and moving up to the scrotum. And you will
pause it there for a few seconds. Well, not on purpose,
of course, because you're a respectful girl, good-natured
and proper. But on your way to getting the coffee you'll
decide to check out the tastes of it, of your invincible rabbit, your warrior and delicacy, your coalminer's lantern
of women's happiness.

Obviously, in such a situation, how can there be any talk of parmesan (*keep in mind that Parmesan is a cat*), cheddar, or, God forbid, mozzarella? Haba will pause, sigh, and place his long arms on your head, but will not be able to resist the sweet suffering for more than a minute, he'll lift you up and toss you onto the bed, under him. And that's it. The pause will conclude. And once again, for seven years, day by day, your *alaindelon* will know nothing about *eau de cologne*, or about learning the Ukrainian language. Because he barely speaks in bed. There's no need to talk anymore about attempts at literary translations between similar languages. There just isn't any time for that, my sunshine, please understand, there just isn't any time.

But after another seven years, keep in mind, he might ask not just for coffee and brie with a tart, but also for a cigarette. Well, now here you figure it out. He is not a demanding guy, let him inhale the blue flame of fate a few times, let him look down at the Kyiv twilight and recall that, besides a hot, otherworldly bosom, the universe also contains stars, a pretty solid imperative (although not categorical enough, perhaps), and the blessed Dnipro River, although it's dirty, like your thoughts are, you whore.

Haba's love rod, his stave, his *bulava* his *bunchuk* and *pirnach*—that wonderful instrument given by God to members of the male sex, in order to find both happiness and trouble— functioned for Haba like a Swiss watch, though sometimes more like a Swiss Army knife.[20] His troubles with women were a whole other story, but we'll get to that later.

So, let us return to the MR. Especially, constantly, and above all, it interested Haba Habinsky as a personality. By the time he was in college, Haba could not fathom where the Ukrainian people got this figure. Why a head? Why the head of a mare? What happened, and why, that made it, alone and concerned, tumble across Europe? And when will it stop tumbling? And what will it do then? If you just stop to think about it, young man, an unspeakable abyss of difficult questions will arise in front of you. The heart will frighten and tighten. You'll realize that it was foolish to have wasted time in your stupid—and useless for this universe—life.

The Beautiful
and the Beneficial

All things are lawful for me, but not all things are beneficial.
All things are lawful for me, but I will not be mastered by anything.
  —The First Epistle of St. Paul to the Corinthians

No one knew or awaited Haba in Kyiv, but no one was banishing him from the city either, which he considered to be a good sign. It's not so much that refugees were feared here, but they were considered to be strangers and therefore treated unkindly. In the days surrounding his arrival, the local newspapers featured many convincing articles in which writers, using just-the-facts, would prove that every refugee was a secret, clandestine, and fully materialized evil that existed solely for the purpose of being defeated, as a means of demonstrating the strength of the Ukrainian spirit and of the holy striving of the nation for freedom and liberty. A refugee from the Donbas could be a separatist, a Russian, a moron, a thief, a pickpocket, a purse-snatcher, a trespasser, a cat-lover, a cat-caller, or even a cat-burglar. He might turn out to have relatives in Moscow, a dependence on alcohol, shingles, and a passion for Chekhov's dramas. Obviously, the continental, naturally noble and clear-eyed Ukraine needed to defend itself from this mob and from the so-called and rather dubious diversity of its own cultural space. And it defended itself as well as it could.

It was difficult to find an apartment and a job. But Haba got lucky. At first, while he still had some of his savings, he made his refugee daily bread working at the city's newspapers and magazines. But when he ran out of money, and it became clear that one can't live exclusively off of philosophy in this city, he found a job at The Beautiful and the Beneficial[1] supermarket. This holder of a PhD was designated as an assistant in two departments—sweets and vegetables. That is, he was responsible for watching over potatoes, cabbage, onions, pickles and tomatoes, sugar beets, powdered sugar, high blood sugar, chocolate, chocolates filled with liqueur, and the eternal and daily *roshen*[2] of the Ukrainian people. In the morning, afternoon, and evening, he was responsible for shuffling carts full of vegetables and sugar to their respective aisles, stacking the products on their shelves, and making sure that there was always enough of them in stock.

The supermarket was tall, like the Hagia Sofia. It was sixty yards tall and the diameter of its central cupola, which on sunny days would shine a cross right over the vegetable and fruit departments, was of almost twenty-five yards. The job didn't pay much, but occasionally you were allowed to take home a bag, or even two, of days-old vegetables and a bit of sugar, which had been moistened by the tears of the Ukrainian people so invisible in the city of Kyiv.

The head manager of various dried fruits, and of the plant world, the former Captain and Soviet-Afghan War veteran, Petsia Petrovych Petrov, was a well-developed, in a metaphysical sense, person. Always slightly buzzed but well-dressed, polite and Ukrainian-speaking, he became an example for Haba of European correctness but also, at the same time, of civil disobedience against the system. That man's most pleasant feature was a natural religious-ness that was not clouded by confessional superstitions. And that is what helped the workers of the supermarket choose the steadfast path to victory when signs of life of the synanthropic species *Rattus* and *Erinaceus europaeus*, representatives of *Sus domestics*, the ubiquitous *Felis silves-tris catus*, and the fabulous *Canis lupus familiaris*—and all kinds of other animals—were discovered in the vegetable and dried fruits departments.

The first to be discovered was *Rattus*. And it was its traces that really worried Haba and Petsia Petrovych. And what kinds of traces? Obviously, not diarrhea.[3] How could diarrhea end up in a prestigious supermarket? It is constructed in such a way that no living creature could sneak into it and eat to one's delight, spend a few days in holy relaxation, and immerse oneself in one's own universe, without being punished. That is why the traces that were discovered, first by Peirulyno and then by Haba, were purely metaphysical and, as such, could not be dis-covered by just anyone. And, of course, not just anyone could choose the proper way to act in the given situation.

What is *Rattus*? Nothing too terrible, generally speak-ing. Any biologist will tell you that. Domain—Eukaryota, kingdom—Animalia, phylum —Chordata, class—Mam-malia, order—Rodentia. But those rats that began entering The Beautiful and the Beneficial basically looked, on the surface, like average Ukrainian citizens. Those very same people, but in the form of rats. What distinguished them, perhaps, was a heightened choleric behavior—sometimes carefully concealed but, nonetheless, obvious—aggressiveness, and a promiscuousness in the means by which they passed along information. To see the rat within a person you need to carefully look into their reflection in the mirror when they don't know that you are looking at them. But seriously, sometimes all you need to do is just talk with them for a bit, check out their Facebook page, bring up the language issue, or ask them to whom Crimea belongs.

In those days when the MR began visiting him, Haba started to see the true essence of people while he traveled with his cart along the difficult, spiritual path between Scylla and Charybdis, between sugar and potatoes. He was not bothered by their exceptional intellect or, let's say, their latest-model cars and three-story condos in fancy new buildings featuring terraces with stunning views of downtown Kyiv. He saw them, well, like we see one another right now—with an internal, silent eye. And he would smile gently, comprehending that he was sent by the Universe to the capital of Ukraine not just for the learning of a language but also for battle and, clearly, for future victory.

The first idea that those two buddies of resistance—the restless Petro Petrakis and Haba—came up with was to let their supervisors know about the rats. But how does one tell the director about them?

For example, you could say, "A family entered. At first, they looked like normal people, but they spoke a strange language, which sounded like rat speak."

The director will then look at you circumspectly and ask: "How do you, Petrusio, know for sure that it was rat speak? Why not calf? Or dog, or cat? And, by the way, how do you know so much about the animal world? Perhaps," he will inquire, "you and Haba are actually two major prophets: you, Petsia are, let's say, Dāwūd, and he's your protégé, Sulaymān?"

***

Piotrek got a bit off track, rubbed his palms together, and looked over at the pouting Haba.

"No, and what the heck does this have to do with Dāwūd and Sulaymān?"

"Because," the director lit a cigarette, poured a bit of whiskey into a glass and offered it to Petro Petrovych (*this will kill your hangover, my boy*), "before Sulaymān, or, if you prefer, Solomon, warriors were made up of genies, people, and birds. And later they were broken up into combat groups."

"Really," Haba said a bit surprised, "people and birds?"

"And genies," the director corrected him. "The thing is, kiddies, that animals—moreover, those that are lovely, like birds—possess both feelings and certain labor skills. Unfortunately," he sighed, "they are not developed enough to be forced to adhere to the Sharia law."

"That's a shame," Pete pondered a bit and downed half a glass of whiskey in one gulp.

"I think they could have been forced to do so," added Haba, "but if it's a Christian raven then let it be a Greek-Catholic one, a Catholic one, or, if need be, an Orthodox one. It could be a follower of the Armenian or Anglican churches (*Oh, black ravens, why do you caw? A difficult question, by the way*), a Jew or a Protestant. And why not? (*Croaked the raven nevermore.*) Kyiv is the Yerusháyim of Europe, isn't it?"

"Ok, let it be Yerusháyim," the director allowed, "but stop it with the squirrels, monkeys, and platinum credit card-wielding rats, or you're going to have to find a different job. Got it?"

When they left their director's office, Haba diverged his belief that it seemed that he and Petrovych were fighting this battle alone.

"And no one will help us, not the directors, nor the full-time employees, let alone the part-time employees."

"That's ok," Perias softly uttered, "there is nothing better than a death that you are ready to accept in honor of your ancestors for the temple of your gods."

"*Natürlich*," Haba agreed, "glory to Ukraine and to its beautiful and beneficial heart."

He was used to trusting Captain Petrenko. For it was this quiet man who gave Haba a job at a time when the latter was down in the dumps (because all of his savings had been spent and he was deeply in debt for his apartment). And it is he who will soon acquaint the refugee with his niece (*nephew?*) Ole-Luk-Oie. And it was Pertos who will one night invite the good old plumber and inventor Vasyl to come to the supermarket to bless the dried fruits and the vegetable aisle. And it is thanks to the very same Ferus that Haba will be able to come out alive after taking part in nationally-esoteric competitions with the mare's head, which should be beginning somewhere in the upcoming pages of this novel.

***

On the other hand, no one can know for sure what will happen next. Especially, in this flawed text. Life is all about improvisation. That is why a sweet sadness narrows your throat when you look up at the Kyiv sky, into the abyss that hovers above the Obolon neighborhood. They move so fast, these clouds, they keep changing their shapes as if they are afraid of pausing, of fully forming. Like a woman who is afraid that her lover will stop moving, that the minty blue explosion, coming after a long, almost five-minute-long yellow-green rhapsody, won't happen. Like a bird or say, a monkey on a tree, that is afraid that the setting sun that it sends off to bed will not appear again tomorrow. But tomorrow will always come. And this scoundrel who syncopates out of exhaustion and drunkenness, ever faster and faster, will finally come. I o-o-o-o! I a-a-a-a!

In other words—happiness.

And the Obolon clouds shout from up high about the happiness of being and rejoicing and swimming above the Ukrainian world, which is full of the heavy smoke of war, sad news, the smells of the McDonald's closest to the metro station, the shouts of grey crows (*Corvus cornix—the lords of Obolon, old inhabitants, the average age of grown birds is so-and-so, wingspan—up to one yard, sometimes—two, a heightened arrogance, the leader of the population—Kazimir the Universal*), and the mysterious rumble of metro trains that tumble in waves underground, reminding daytime Kyiv of the eternal darkness of history, which forms in front of our eyes and your eyes, but then, almost never becomes the subject of everyday concerns, of morning-time orgasms, of fleeting memories, of constant deadlines, of new short stories, and of kids, who, thank God, are continuously born in this land.

***

"Her name is Ole-Luk-Oie," said Petsia Petrovych after they each drank another mug of dark beer. "I would guess that she's about seventeen or eighteen years old, so please be delicate with her. She may not be well-versed in everything but she's a good girl. Also, her mom passed away when the girl was ten. And she never knew her father. I am her only guardian and confidant."

"Listen, captain," Haba coughed out, "I don't think this is one of your better ideas."

Piotrek ate a couple slices of smoked pig ears and burped loudly.

"What's the problem? Doesn't the fact that I got you this job count for something?"

"Yes, of course," Haba smiled sluggishly, "of course, it does."

"So then, what's the problem?"

Haba pondered for a bit and took another sip. The Kyiv sun was tumbling down outside the window and, beyond it, the city's naturally fluid time melted into space. The space blinked, mumbled something with doll-like little lips, and wrapped itself in drawn-out rows of visual text that floated in the sky above the city in clean, dark stanzas. The rays of the sun dissolved the text and some of the letters partially dripped into the Dnipro, partially dropped onto the shore, onto the bridges, roofs, and landing stages, onto restaurants, hydroparks, onto the holy Kyiv Pechersk Lavra, onto Podil, onto St. Michael's Square.

"Hey, did you doze off?" Petro pushed the table of snacks towards Haba. "Eat something—we've been drinking since noon."

"The thing is, captain," Haba coughed out, "that I have not had a great track record with women." Having taken another gulp of beer, he once again lit up a smoke and then glanced into Petro's blue eyes.

"So what?"

"What do you mean, so what?" Habinsky jerked his shoulders, "it would be better if you offered your Olia-Luk-Oie to a different refugee, so that he could prepare her for a grand and futile meeting with the academic world, with astrolophites and ascetomasters, aerosanites and aerophones, bakhtomasters and balancers, metal morons and energy inducers.

"Energy inducers," Petro Petrovych repeated, deep in thought.

"Yes," Haba nodded, "let somebody else introduce her to the world of bas reliefs and bannisters, of modulations and stagnations, explain to her how monastery vaults are built, in what ways an arch bridge differs from a bow-beam bridge, how statue marble differs from rock marble, or, let's say, how fool's gold differs from that which is used to cover Kyiv churches. Because I'll tell you right away: when I begin getting to know a person, if she is a woman, or, let's say, a girl, it doesn't really matter, in the metal framework of my coalminer's nature a certain electrostimulation occurs, and nothing good has ever come of it. Trust me, it is better not to experiment. At least the previous few times, as far as I remember, everything turned out to be too original, to put it nicely, too peculiar. I barely came out of it alive. I don't want to, my friend, regardless of the fact that I desperately need to socially immerse myself and make acquaintances in this strange, beautiful and ethereal—taking into account my background—world of Kyivan meta-Ukrainian beyond-existence. Because it's unnatural at my age to only count as my friends, besides you, Mrs. Potato, Mr. Onion, Mrs. Ketchup, and Mr. Zuckerberg. There is something bad about that."

Petsia downed some beer and smiled at Haba.

"A stubborn mule is a wolf's prey."

"What are you trying to say?"

"Don't even think about it," the captain explained." "Olia-Luk-Oie is not the kind of girl that can easily be lured in anyway. You'll see," Piotrek lit up a cigarette, inhaled some smoke, and slowly exhaled it, carefully staring right at the little bonfire that burned at the end of the cigarette. "Olia is an angel. I can't say for sure but, perhaps even the angel of death. So, honestly, I don't envy you if you've really thought about doing something like that. You have to understand, she's an orphan and that is why, since childhood, in order to defend herself from bad people, she had to learn all sorts of Karate, Qu Yuan, Bushido, One-Do, Yosa no Buson, Ariwara No-Narihira, Sun Yue-Yue, Li Houzhu-Yue, Siu Mai, Thai-Gu, Buniano Asuka, Tai Chi Tsiu, etc. And keep in mind, I've listed only what I am able to recall after my fifth beer."

"Holy moly," Habinsky said earnestly, bringing the beer to his lips.

"Not 'holy moly' but 'holy muscovite'," the captain instructively yawned, inhaled, looked up and exhaled and slapped Haba on the back. "That said, if something should develop between the two of you, then I would be fine with that. Although we have not known one another very long, we are almost like family now. So, do not be concerned at all. Speak freely, feel freely, rid yourself of any unnecessary metaphysical stress, feel light and relaxed, be like the wind in the pine needles of the Publiieve-Neronove nature reserve, like a nice free bird, like a nationally-conscious rabbit, wise and undefeatable."

"I get the rabbit part but why did you mention it with regards to speaking?"

"No reason," Petsia replied immediately and finished his beer. "Are you seeing a psychiatrist?"

"Regularly," Haba offered and silenced in deep thought.

A sweet and dreamy smoke swam above their heads, taking up unexpected forms. Haba, for instance, saw drawings on the ceiling of the kitchen where they were sitting that were similar to those made by Michelangelo in 1508–1512.

"What you've got here isn't a kitchen but the Sistine Chapel," Habinsky noted, outlining with his cigarette the cycle of frescos that to this day are considered to be the best masterpieces of High Renaissance art. They shone above their heads, slowly circled and, it seems, even gave off a pleasant, quiet music. Perucho gently laughed.

"Well, aren't you funny and delightful. Like a crazy sparrow."

"Funny?" Haba lowered his shoulders, "I'm not funny at all, it's the other way around—a grown man in the culmination of his own zen."

"You're going to talk to me about zen?" The captain ate a piece of an ear, smiling at Haba gently and quietly. "Don't you worry about a thing. Take care of yourself first. And make it so that my little girl will finally get her share, and I don't care what path she takes. What's more important is that she gets on that route and sets off along it. And where it leads to is not my concern. What's key in life is to travel along your chosen path where it leads you and not to worry too much about where it is exactly leading. Anyway, it's none of your business. You just move, don't change direction, look ahead, breath in rhythm, don't drink booze until the afternoon, read the Bible, or at least anything at all, grab life by the tits, bite them, chew, scream from pain or from joy, get the stressed syllable, the suffixes, and the endings right. Reflect. Do breathing exercises. Believe in the *vyrii*.[4] (*My poor head, // Left the* vyrii *early, // Snow covers the mountains, // Water fills the valleys*.)[5] That's a short program for beginners. An algorithm, so to say, for growing older. The rest will come."

Haba became pensive.

"And what's a *vyrii*? Sorry, I've just begun learning the Ukrainian language."

"It's paradise, the heavens—the *vyrii* lies on the other side of the sea, or on an island in the middle of the sea. Most probably in the middle of the Dnipro river. The Sun comes to this island having completed its daily journey over the Andriivskyi descent. You may find it hard to believe, but there, near the saint Lavra, an eternal summer reigns."

"Keep going," Haba chuckled.

"That's how it is. Or course, everything there is green, beautiful, and surprisingly beneficial. And when the harsh winter begins in Kyiv, or a reactionary, anti-Ukrainian government arrives on Bankova Street,[6] it is precisely there that nature's life goes to hide for the time being: birds fly in, all kinds of seeds are stashed away, Kozaks and kobzars,[7] four oxen and eight elephants, upon which the Ukrainian universe stands, the grey hares of our knowledge, and the lord of the subconscious Hermes Trismegistus can be found there. This is where the virtual matrix formed by our ancestors and the souls of the people who have not yet been born in Ukraine is located. And they must be born. Though, perhaps, they don't really want to be."

"The souls of those who have not yet been born. That's strange. And what does the soul of your niece desire?"

"Well, who the heck knows," the captain shook his head. "If I knew, I would have helped her with that a long time ago. But that is your main assignment, to determine who she is and what her path is. I do know that she likes to read."

"And what does she read?" Haba asked with interest.

"Books, of course," the captain twitched his shoulders.

"Yes," Haba nodded his head, "I understand, first I need to meet Olia and then we can make scholastic arrangements."

"Exactly! You see how quickly you pick up on everything!" The captain slapped his palm on the table out of satisfaction. "Because you are a refugee! People here are more contemplative, restrained, measured, it's as if they've been slowed by ancient space and time. While you," Pietrania stood up from the table and looked at the large clock hanging above the door, "are completely different. It's as if you just came into the world. Quick and easily engaged. Like a shadow on the ice. That's it. The master of blessing, the handyman of blessing will be near the supermarket in a half an hour. It is now time for us to go."

"But won't the security guards get in our way?" Haba located the pack of cigarettes and the lighter with his hands and put them in his pocket.

"Our conscience is our security, *mon chéri*," Pierre sternly declared. "Let's go—quickly."

"Why quickly?"

"So that we don't be tempted by the beer. Beer is beer, it's not kerosene."

"What do you think," Haba enumerated, once they had already gone out into the autumn Kyiv space, "are we going to bless the Beautiful and the Beneficial or not?"

"I don't know if we'll bless everything that is beautiful and beneficial in the world," Petrunio paused by the doors, "because we love the work that transforms into creativity,[8] but there is no doubt about the vegetable and dried fruits departments. And then we'll see how it goes. Vasyl and I believe that this is only the beginning of our battle with those whom we cannot mention here."

"Yes, because it's creepy to do so," Haba tossed in.

"And this Vasyl, who visited me at home," Petro Petrovych added, "I've known him since I was a kid. He's from the same village as I am, he's amazing, much more impressive than me and you. An inventor, a hermit, a patriot. You will definitely become friends. You'll see, he said that he would first visit his acquaintance, a nun, for a blessing—an erstwhile lover is a holy thing—and then he promised to come by the store. I'll put it this way—once Vasyl has decided to bless something then he'll bless it. He's a persistent dude. And God will help him. God is not a lamb, he sees everything.[9] It's time to go."

***

At this point, it is unclear how to make the MR the central character in this story, because we've talked about it a lot, but it's still somewhere over there, up ahead of this flippant and inept narrative. And we don't know how we should proceed. But it's better not to know anything (*we are, in fact, no Descartes*), but instead simply visit Haba on a day when he is off from work, which may have already taken place at this moment in our story, or, conversely, is still to come. With this Kyiv time, you never know which day it is that people live in. Is it the one that has just passed, in which case we can feel a bit calmer? Or is it the one that is still waiting for us, somewhere ahead in our endless and eternal life?

But forget about that. Habinsky is lying on the floor and looking out the window. He has several dreams—strange, long-lasting, action-packed, and refined. He saw his past. This is a difficult challenge because, like all pasts, the past that Haba dreamed about requires immediate responses to questions that it poses. And all of this is made additionally complicated because that past, which Haba saw, never existed. Or did it?

He lies on the floor. The wind and the sky. And he might even be crying; that's how it seems at first glance. It's not a moisture of catharsis or of a long and endless pain. It's the moisture of insanity, because only it allows that which did not take place to leave, only it recreates that which you cannot remember. So, what is in those eyes that are aimed at the sky and at the clouds? What is that delicate, bloody, tousled like a three-day rose, and salty from tears, forty-nine-year-old Kyiv rabbit Haba Habinsky thinking about?

Maybe he is thinking about two beautiful girls that once lived in eastern Ukraine. One, for example, had the name Snavduliia and the other one Sosipatra. At this moment, Haba cannot remember which one he loved, or whether he ever loved either one of them. Whether they are two people or one woman, a universal one. God knows. Memory doesn't really preserve such things. Because it's not clear what it should preserve. Developed individuals who freely travel along the text of existence know perfectly well: memories, as places where some sort of archival documents are stored on shelves, do not exist. Our whole life is entirely just the flickering of the heart and is completely based on fantasies and transformations. On language, to be more precise. That is why the past, as you recall it, is always hastily assembled.

For example, it is necessary to recall the first time he had sex.

Ok, as you wish, my friend. And a not-very-sober editor jumps out from the storeroom of the brain—brother Hermes Trismegistus—sits behind the mixing board and, in three milliseconds, edits your memories in the way that they are.

On the screen is the face of the dreamy chemistry teacher and her skirt. Her thighs, buttocks, and breasts. The sun shines on her hair turning it into a yellow flame.

Her narrow palms. Her long pink fingers tremble as she closes the laboratory, where you remain face to face with fate, with a warm, albeit completely worn out by generations of school children, rug, with the scents of manganese and iodine, litmus and oxygen, fuel tablets and ammonium nitrate, potassium carbonate, deoxyribonucleic and ribonucleic love, etc.

And, eventually, bees and clouds, test tubes and beakers, begin to clang and dance. Metallurgical factories within a radius of sixty miles and multicolored laboratory flasks radiate a sweet and suffocating death. Gas pipes glow. Glass stirring rods and tubes slowly rise from their places and head westward, creating Amedeo Modigliani's portraits of women with their movement. Kipp's apparatus transforms into a fancy hookah, while, outside the window, a sudden rain is threatening and a wind rustles in the simmering poplars.

An alcohol burner, an electric sphere with a stand for test tubes, an electric stove, and gas burners all recite Mendeleev's chart, a small metal laboratory spoon hops into your hand and you're able to use it to start a fire. A damp hot flame eats out your eyes. The test tube stand imitates the sexual act with the crucible tongs. The asbestos screen expands to the dimensions of the Messier galaxy. And you do know, oh how well you know, that spiral galaxy in the Ursa Major constellation. Its diameter is so-and-so light-years and its brightness so-and-so. The distance between the chemistry teacher's vagina and this boundless giant is forty-five million light-years. Mommy dearest, what a distance, what happiness! Every kid in this laboratory understands that you can gaze at it (*not the vagina, of course, the galaxy*) all spring. It's so wonderful, it's so pertinent and so obvious to everybody who knows that its coordinates are as such: so-and-so degrees—orbital inclination; so-and-so hours and so-and-so minutes—direct insertion.

Oh! You now know everything about direct and indirect insertion. And insertion and extraction and an endless list of various movements.

Your lover either laughs or cries, or gently groans, like the wind in the branches of the autumn acacias, when the final, cold September rains lead an amusing and transparent October by the hand. It is in such Octobers that a playful school-time love, destined for eternity, is born. And it is these yellow leaves and these drunk chestnuts that make a tender and ashamed thirty-year-old woman somehow take the hand of her own student and lead him into the holiest of holy in the whole world of chemistry right before your eyes.

And who is he? A standard Nobody. Just a boy. Quiet, always keeps to himself, very skinny. He loves the singing of the wind in the autumn trees, sour apples, the yellow moon, and the green stars. In general, he eschews attention and arrives thirty-forty minutes early for the first class because he lives in the suburbs. He is always afraid of being late and he doesn't like his fellow classmates or this cement box in which he spends his little life.

There is a lack of spaciousness within these walls. Within these veins. There is too little oxygen in the school's air. And maybe it is because of this lack of oxygen, which, strangely enough, is a manifestation of that—uncontrollable by the school schedule—desire to breathe and to live, that she takes him by the hand. She leads him to think that she will tell this little Avogadro

Amedeo, this sweet Arrhenius Svante August, this un-matched Gay-Lussac, about everything, the whole truth. And she'll even show it to him.

He and she are facing one another. It's a hazy shot. The colors have slowed, softened. Lots of fiery-yellow and red. The frame—bronze and brass. No one hears, no one looks, no one realizes, and, in the end, no one speaks. The teacher touches the face of her young scientist with long pink nails, caressing his neck, arms, and legs. It is as if she is showing this youth how the human organism is constructed, which parts of it are the most important, and why precisely adult life does not anticipate happiness. This silent lesson cannot last long because, as you can guess, awaiting them is a path in search of that special stone, from which gold, cooper, a tear, and fire are born.

It begins in October and lasts until springtime. And then the horrible period of summer arrives. Skłodowska Curie has to travel with her husband to a Truskavets spa for a holiday. She has issues with her kidneys, and she needs to drink water that is filled with something that is beneficial, though it is not very beautiful. (*Truskavets mineral waters—the best not only in Ukraine, but also all over the word. It is true, however, that some of the springs have a certain characteristic—the smell of sperm and natural gas, the bitter taste of death and almond.*)

Over a period of time, this is what will end up killing her. A basic operation to remove the philosopher's stone from her kidneys will render the young, delicate instructor of chemical love and loving chemistry dead at age thirty-two. A sad Haba won't be able to get himself to visit her grave until three months after her burial when he arrives with a bottle of sweet, putrid wine, which he drinks straight from the bottle, and a bouquet of pure white and blue flowers, which he tore out of the abandoned lot by the church. This will be the first wine (*what a nasty taste*) of his life and his first (*his own*) death.

The film that Hermes Trismegistus unravels clatters, clicking its black tongue, rambles, sings (*tongue, tongue, evil will render you undone*).[10] You stare at the scenes, you rewind, you can't believe it. Hermes, what are you doing. You've lost your mind. A ghost and an illusion. I couldn't have had such a lover. And at such a young age. Haba and I are only about twelve–thirteen years old. The door to the balcony is open, an abyss into the sky. Children and birds shout. The wind strolls about the rooms.

Memory is a peculiar and funny little thing, which belongs to a different person, who has lived in an unseen world, each time. And this person no longer exists, and no longer will there be a life or world like that and, honestly, there never was. Well then, what was there? Something, nonetheless, took place with us over a certain period of years. Maybe not just with you and me, not just with us and, probably, not just in this life. But still, that something had a place and that place had certain coordinates. No?

In life, like in rye, time quickly goes by. It is easy to forget what pipettes, burettes, flasks, cylinders, beakers, crucibles, evaporating dishes, and mortars and pestles your first lover liked. This is especially true of the pestles. Because she understood pestles like no one else. O those mortars, o those pestles. An eternal desire to mix and pound.

***

Habinsky finally climbed to the top of Golden Gates. The twenty-ninth station of the Kyiv metro. Although it's raining, there are many people by the metro. It's always like that here. The Syretsko-Pechersk Line. Dark-blue clumps crawl in the sky. They formed over the Baltics and swam over here to this station, which has existed since December 31st of the eighty-ninth year of the previous century in order to ruin people's moods. This sense of dampness kills one's self-confidence. And it is only the round columns, the Byzantine chapiters, and the mosaic panels, only the eternal dark-grey granite, that somehow support the will to movement, if not to work. According to *The Daily Telegraph*, it is one of the twenty-two most beautiful subway stations in Europe. Kyi, Shchek, Khoryv, Lybid, Dyr, Askold, Ihor Son of Rurik, the esteemed Princess Olha, and so on, all the way up to Danylo Romanovych. In other words, all of our guys and gals are here, everyone is where they are supposed to be, there is no need for any concern. Your insanity will find you, nonetheless. And there's the St. Sophia Cathedral, and there's the Church of the Tithes, oh and there we have the Irynine Church, and, hey look—it's St. Michael's Church. St. Cyril's Church, The Mother of God Church at Pyrohoshcha, The Church of the Saviour at Berestove. Some say that Orthodoxy brought nothing but grief to the people of Kyiv. It doesn't look that way. The griffins, at least, came out really good. They are so frickin' awesome.

Just look at them. One is Halibei, the other Babliuk. Some people believe that they are named Begma and Bedzyk, but that's crazy. They respond only to Halibei and Babliuk. Although it is true that Babliuk sometimes thinks he's Halibei and that Halibei stubbornly associates himself with Babliuk. You say—Halibei, sweetheart, come to me. But nope, he doesn't. He squirms. Overindulged medieval bastard.

Haba loved those beasts, because griffins, obviously, are completely mythical creatures: each of them is both an eagle and a lion. Like all the world's refugees, these beasts are completely irresponsible and, on evenings such as this one, helpless too. And what's the deal with a griffin? What's he all about? A tail that is long and fabulous. In this case, for some reason, triangular. A character that is playful, quirky. And there you have it—a griffin. Babliuk is convinced that his being personifies the Sun, strength, and the astuteness of wisdom. Halibei is responsible for the swiftness of punishment and retribution. In Haba's first months in Kyiv, he would play with them for long periods of time, feed those poor dudes poppy-seed buns, which he would buy at Iaroslavna and, eventually, they began recognizing him.

The meeting was set up on Iaroslaviv Val, in that very same Iaroslavna café, where they sell poppy-seed buns and coffee, wine, cognac, and compote. The lampposts flickered. People hurried. Smiling faces swam about. The Baltic clouds created a peacefulness and a slow and dull light rain. The young, the old, the Ukrainian-speaking and the English-speaking, everyone was happy for some reason. There is no doubt that among them were readers of James Augustine Aloysius Joyce. And this was a bit strange. How are they able to read such wise books when, in the world—that is, in the Ukrainian world—there's a war going on, or, as they say, an ATO endures?[11]

Haba never really understood what this ATO means. Perhaps it stands for "authentic types of observation." But what does that have to do with the war in the east? What about that merciless death that collects its harvest in these lands? What about the despair that smolders in one's heart and does not disappear, even in dreams? In conscious dreams, Habinsky would ever more frequently end up in a strange place, in the same one with which he became familiar back in those final Donetsk months. There, people and dolls had equal rights. It was a complete horror, but in no ways was it an ATO. And, if it is about observation, then why is there this constant pain that eats at your insides and squeezes out, not only dish and fish or hook and rook, but also realty itself, from your brain.

But really, it's all quite clear. The Ukrainian government is developing skills in the selection and schematization of observation of characteristics. Any Leonardo da Vinci worth his salt must master the skill of simplifying a characteristic in order to later squeeze it into his own talented individuality. These methods have existed for ages. Almost since prehistoric times. It was Schiller who noticed that aesthetic and creative aspirations would constitute a joyous kingdom of play and safety amidst a grave world. It's as if it frees people from everything that hounds them in both the physical and psychological sense. And that is where ATO comes from. Generalization and schematization—those are the two poles upon which we have been hung, my brother. And we dangle, tangle, and sway from there, kinda like two happy scarecrows among the corn. Painted faces, rags blackened by the rains and winds and, instead of hearts, which were eaten-out by the occupiers—there is a poplar stick. The birds jeer at the scarecrow, the roads beckon and lure, but where can he really go now, one-legged, damaged, and poor? And a frickin' Russian-speaking one at that. Sorry, gentlemen, if that last bit doesn't rhyme.

Looking around the room, Haba didn't see the person with whom he was supposed to meet. On the one hand, the verbal portrait painted by Petro Petrenko may not really reflect reality. But that's not a problem. In real life, Haba looked just like he did on his Facebook page—gloomy and lackluster.

"If she wants to find me, she'll find me," he said to himself and got some compote, cognac, and a poppy-seed bun, hung up his leather jacket on the back of a chair, and once again looked around. Iaroslavna quietly rocked on the waves of time. People swam past it. Flowing past the large windows were the street, the buildings across it, stars, cars, female smiles, and past life, and circling around all of this was the ATO zone, like Jupiter around the sun.

"Let our doll not forsake us,[12]" Haba said, lifted the cognac, smelled it, felt the sweet aroma of genuine Transcarpathia and took a gulp. The liquid turned out to be so pleasant that he couldn't resist and drank up everything that he had purchased. He thought about it and got another portion of that thick, fragrant amber.

"I believe you're the one that I am looking for," a joyful, young bell rang just above his right ear.

Haba breathed in the air, which still had the aroma of cognac and carefully turned his head. A smallish, young woman in light-grey overalls and a green coat. He wrapped his chosen one in the coat of his love,[13] thought Haba, got up and bowed.

"Habinsky!"

"Ole-Luk-Oie," the girl gave her name and sat down on the stool across from Haba.

"What can I get you?" Habinsky gallantly smiled. "Coffee, compote, green-black tea, a *pliatsok*, a bun, or some chocolate?"[14]

"Get me some cognac, too, please," Ole acquiesced, "and a big mug of black tea."

"Of course, as you wish," Haba lowered his shoulders, "but would Uncle Petrusio approve?"

"Oh, don't worry about that," the girl chuckled, "I'm no longer twenty years old, I am allowed to have sweets."

Haba ordered cognac and poppy-seed buns for the girl and for himself, waited for the server to pour boiled water into the mug and thought about the fact that Ole had turned out to be quite different than he had imagined. It seems that Petrusio was mistaken. After his conversation with his friend, Haba had expected a delicate and shy, yet very serious eighteen-year-old girl. And here, my friends, we have at least a twenty-year-old, or even, gasp, a twenty-three or a twenty-four year-old! (*twenty-five?*) And she is by no means shy. A young, attractive woman. Fairly happy eyes, a trim figure, cool overalls, a somewhat juvenile little coat, and a pink umbrella. And on top of all that—she drinks cognac. "Well, for God's sake, what is left for me to teach her?" Haba pondered.

"Let us drink to our acquaintance," the girl suggested. "Uncle has told me much about you. He said that you are a serious, honest, highly educated, Ukrainian-language-speaking person. You can tell the difference between *banosh* and *zupa* and, in general, you have some kind of degree."[15]

"Really?" Haba made himself smaller, "To be honest, your uncle is exaggerating. Ok, I got *banosh* down, but I am not all that well-versed in *zupa* as I would like to be, it's difficult without practice."

"But aren't you a scholar?"

"The scholarliest scholar," Haba smiled. "To be honest, I agreed to meet you only because, in those couple of months (*days? years?*) that we've worked together, Petro Petrovych has become almost like family for me. At the same time, I really have no idea in what context our future relationship could develop, if it is to develop at all."

"Understood," Ole smiled. "How about a brief course in literary aesthetics? You specialize in that, don't you?"

"And what use does a woman your age have for that?" Haba honestly inquired.

Ole once again laughed.

"Forgive me," he became concerned, "I didn't mean to say that young women have no need for this, what I..."

"Don't fret," Luk-Oie suggested, lifting the glass of cognac. "Shall we drink to our acquaintance?"

"Yes, indeed," Habinsky agreed.

He drank up and inhaled the air that was filled with the din and the smells of the buffet and looked through the windows of Iaroslavna. On the opposite side, above the chaotic and multi-colored crowd, emerged the silhouette of the MR. Its eyes were sad and distressed. It smoked, as always, a slim cigarette and one could see in its eyes that it was not feeling very well. It's not used to having people around, Haba thought with pity, it's always alone, doesn't know anyone in the city besides me and, on top of all that, there's the traumatic experience of authentic observation. Something needs to finally be done with this.

"What are you looking at?" Ole became interested and began eating the poppy-seed bun.

"It's nothing," Haba lowered his shoulders and turned his eyes away from the window. "A familiar figure flashed by. So, you say you want to become a student? What subject are you interested in? I assume that technical studies are not really your thing, right? And that's a good thing because technical studies and I are not a good match..."

"The thing is," Ole placed her unfinished bun on the plate, "that I'm already in my second year as a PhD student at Chernivtsi University. I'm hoping to defend my dissertation next year."

Haba paused for a minute. He once again looked through the window. The Mare's Head had disappeared. The wind was picking up, but the Baltic clumps hadn't gone anywhere. They blackened, blued, and circled above the city, and it became clear that the rain wouldn't stop until morning.

"Honestly, at this point I don't understand anything. Then why am I here? What's the point?"

"The point is," Luk-Oie cheerfully explained, "that Uncle Petro believes that his niece is now brainy enough and that the time has come for her to be happy."

"In the matrimonial sense of the word?"

"Of course," she nodded her head and laughed jovially. "But don't worry. That's what my uncle thinks, not me."

"You don't want to be happy?" Haba inquired seriously.

"I am happy. Everything is fine."

"So, what are we to do then?" Haba shrugged his shoulders. "Why did we meet, why are we drinking this cognac? In times of war, humanities scholars need to have a clear understanding of their own motives, their consequences, and the reasons for them."

"You know," Ole giggled, "my uncle always tries to introduce me to people, but I don't want to meet with most of them. And when he told me about you christening the dried fruit, I truly became interested. Besides, I was free for the evening, and so I decided that it was no big deal."

Luk-Oie became quiet, checked out the elder couple by the neighboring table for a few seconds, took a sip of tea and a bite of the *pliatsok*.

"What do you say?"

At first, Haba said nothing, just ate a small piece of the bun and then remarked: "The way I see it, he asked me to 'instruct' you, but you don't need any instruction, and he told you that I'm insane and that I need to talk to someone. Correct? That's what bugs me about Petro, his constant tending to me. One cannot deprive a Kyivite of his absolute disrespect for the internal brittle world of a displaced person."

"You misunderstood..."

"I already told him," Habinsky could feel how in the depths of his multi-eyed "I" the Bee of Great Anger was lifting its head, "that I am not crazy. Moreover, I regularly visit my psychiatrist, so everything is fine. Except that my head hurts sometimes. But that should be of no concern to anyone..."

Haba had become sweaty (*a worm is the larva of an insect*), the smile and silvery eyeglasses of Laurentius shone before him. Grabbing his head (*that lives in the ground*), he exerted great efforts in holding himself back. Accursed war. (*St. Nicholas has turned to dust because of the worms. And even the savior himself, the one on the gates, has split in half.*)[16]

"But I thought it was so funny!" Luk-Oie added, glancing straight into Habinsky's eyes and touching his damp palm, and, in doing so, instantly chasing away the intruding unpleasant reality. "It's so great that you and Uncle Petro are friends, oh my god, Mr. Habinsky, blessed onions and dill, that's awesome!"

"Really?" Haba smiled at his cognac, took a big gulp (*no one will end up falling on the floor and yelling*) and, attempting to act as quietly as possible, took his hands off the table and began secretly rubbing his palms on his pant legs.

"This is so hilarious, oh my god," Ole jovially laughed. "Moliere and Beaumarchais have got nothing on you. Three grown men in a drunken state christening a store. That is just precious."

"Yep," Haba nodded, "The Eleusinian Mysteries."

***

The Beautiful and the Beneficial is part of the KarmaTown shopping-entertainment center. That huge, silent, and lively space greeted Petro Petrakis and Haba with the smells of a mopped-up floor, of air still filled with the perfume that is sold in the daytime by its entrance, of tasty hot corn on the cob that was cooked right here by the cash registers of the Beautiful and the Beneficial an hour or two ago, and of the light and romantic, like one's first love, smells of onion, cabbage potatoes, bananas, kiwis, and fresh but not quite ripe mandarins. A realm of soft, subdued light.

During the day—it is true—in this giant space, which is as big as St. Peter's Church in Rome, there are two hundred forty or, more likely, three thousand three hundred thirty-two, different enterprises. Thirty-four of them or, probably, fifty-eight, are restaurants, bars, cafes, or small, simple fast-food stands. Five hundred forty are clothing and jewelry shops. Seventy-three are stores with souvenirs or household goods. Eighteen—bank offices. Ten—toy stores, adult ones too. Five are shops with European cheeses and wines. The second and third floors are set aside for leisure.

"This is your first time here, right Vasyl? Wait until you see it," Petro smiled with glee. "Altogether, the center takes up an X number of thousands of square feet or, one hundred five square miles. Which, by the way, is equal to the size of a city such as Paris."

"In other words, it's big enough," Vasyl respectfully nodded.

"Plenty. Besides The Beautiful and the Beneficial, we've got bowling-shmowling, a pool with dolphins, tennis with rackets," Petro poured silent Haba and good Vasyl some vodka, "an ice-skating rink to sense the coldness of existence, a small private zoo, three movie theaters with movies, a theater floating on water, a cabaret, fourteen slick business centers and beautifully-equipped halls for assemblies. In other words, assembly halls."

"Truly convenient." Vasyl drank a shot of vodka and ate a pickle.

"Yep," Petro agreed. "In one try you can get a vacuum-cleaner, take a selfie with a monkey, drink some whiskey, go for a swim in a pool, drink some whiskey, insure your life, play a few rounds of tennis, drink some whiskey, and then after all that, like a true man, get on the skating rink and fucking kill yourself."

"It's really, really convenient," Haba nodded, "all this place needs is a funeral parlor."

"In general, I think," Petro continued, "what we really need here is an open natal pavilion."

"A 'Quasimodo' natal pavilion, a 'Nie ma sprawy' funeral parlor, a Prometheus crematorium, and a Nestor Makhno TV-radio station," Haba emended.[17]

"Yes," Petrunio agreed, "and we're unswervingly moving in that direction."

The posse quieted down and, without agreeing to do so, all started going in the direction of huge glass doors almost five meters tall through which one could see cars racing along an avenue, stopping at red lights; they looked at the large buildings of new residential complexes, which had just lit up with the happy hearths of family joy and comfort, and they observed the endless life of a big, strange city: the capital of a country at war.

The Beautiful and the Beneficial takes up less than twenty percent of KarmaTown's first floor. At night, you can just sit on the floor, like now, and listen to how all those things that fill up the Obolonian Paris live. You can hear how Turkish gold converses with Chinese jumble, how an indiscernible individual knocks a ping-pong ball on bare, tennis tables, whose green backs extend to the horizon where, exhausted by the monotony of life, the sad killer whale, Femida, who has for two years already been presented by this attraction's owners as the dolphin Tolia, swims in a large dark pool lit up by the fires of Obolon. And this Femida is in no way a Tolia and, moreover, not a dolphin. It is a killer whale, *Orcinus orca*, hailing from a population of the Norwegian Sea that specializes in herring and follows the migration of the latter to the shores of Norway every autumn. And it is because of its love for herring, and not for those loud, stupid creatures that come to KarmaTown every day, that it has not eaten any of them. It swims and senses the whole city living and dancing, and dying, and crying, and laughing around it. And it doesn't like it because it does not understand how one can live like that. How one can eat herring that was frozen a hundred years ago and is sold at The Beautiful and the Beneficial and, on top of that, is chased with shots of cheap Polish vodka?

And beneath this random junk, beneath Femida, beneath The Beautiful and the Beneficial, beneath these dudes, who are sitting on the floor by the stands and discussing life, the subway pulses along towards nighttime. This pulse is constantly felt. But soon the hour will come when the underground world will shut its doors. The metro-beast needs time to digest today's impressions and the living shadows of slapdash people, their smiles and memory, and their pictures and movements, that will remain in distant and endless undergrounds for eternity.

Haba thought about all of this while Vasyl talked about how he once studied in a monastery, how he met his first wife, then left the priesthood, and then went to work at a factory. He became the talented head of a division, a great plumber, a big-time dreamer with a capital "D," and then he graduated from a college, became the constructor of constructors, a businessman, even had a few patents, whatever that means. But he stayed true to the hobbies of his youth. He loved to read the Bible and ponder his future meeting with Christ. He travelled to Jerusalem several times, to the Garden Tomb, to see what is there and what had happened there with his own eyes. He cried like a child when he saw the Garden of Gethsemane (*And then Jesus came with them to the place known as Gethsemane and said to His disciples*). And, in everyday life, he always found time to instruct and heal with enlightening lessons the toiling hearts of the proletariat and managers of this world.

"Shall we begin, boys?" he finally said, and Peter, with Haba in tow, seemed to have awoken from a long sleep.

"You sure are a good storyteller, my dear Vasyl," Petrunio rocked his head and glanced at the clock above the entrance, "maybe you should have indeed become a priest. Maybe we would have already had Heaven on earth for some time now."

"Would have gotten God's blessing for Ukraine," Haba added, "and would've moved it a bit to the left."

"Where to the left?" Vasyl couldn't understand.

"Past Poland, at least. Let the Poles deal with the Russians on their own. And then we'd see who Lviv belongs to and what authentic national memory looks like. Or, even better—past Germany. Let us have a border with the Benelux countries. With all of them at once, at that."

They became quiet.

"Now then," Vasyl said at last.

All three of them got up. They mused for a bit. Petro rubbed his beard and motioned to Vasyl.

"Begin!"

Vasyl pulled out of his bag that which he brought with him, laid out everything on the stools, and made the sign of the cross.

"In the name of the Father, of the Son, and of the Holy Spirit!" He said with a regular voice and coughed. He then read a few Psalms, prayers to God the Father, to the Holy Spirit and to Mother of God. "We are blessing the dried fruits of The Beautiful and the Beneficial," he proclaimed at last, sternly looking somewhere into the otherworld space, "and through it—the whole plant world of Ukraine, consumer goods for the soul and body, white sugar and strong onions, buckwheat, Thai rice, the citizen's spirit, all of our salt and soda, and oil. And together with them, chocolate, cocoa beans, nuts, various seeds, salted pork, and vodka. Let coffee be not bitter, but let tea, pepper, and all types of ginger (medicinal, *Zingiber officinale*) be so. Amen."

"Why all that?" Habinsky commented unsatisfyingly. "We have no desire to bless vodka and meat. We desire only that dried fruits be blessed."

"Drop it," Piotrek grabbed Haba by the sleeve of his sweater, "he knows what he should and shouldn't say. Let him say it. It's working out alright, isn't it? Keep in mind, Hitler was an abstinent and vegetarian specter."

"Let these holy goods not be touched by the gluttonous hand of an evil beast," Vasyl continued, "that is—by its nails, claws, talons, or hooks. Let neither alien overseas wisdom nor our local metaphysical evil ruin the holy and beneficial God's plan to make everything around us magnificent and wonderful. Let these dry and beneficial raisins, cherries, prunes, dates, pears, apples, ginger, and pitted apricots..."

"Raisins and dried apricots with pits," Haba suggested.

"Raisins and dried apricots with pits," Vasyl picked up and ran with it, "dried mushrooms and condensed milk, preserves, jams, jellies, and powdered eggs all be blessed, grow and multiply."

Haba approached the stand where an unopened bottle of vodka stood, grabbed it, carefully looked around, sat on the floor, and took a few sips.

"And let this war finally come to an end," he said quietly.

"Vasyl, let this war come to an end!" Petro asked.

"Merciful God!" Vasyl yelled as tears involuntarily began to fill his eyes. "Let this war, which denies us peace and rest, end. Forgive us, God, have mercy on us!"

Having said that, he pulled out candles, which he had brought with him from the Holy Land, from the Church of the Holy Sepulchre, lit them and stuck one or two of them into a potato, a few into oranges and kiwis, seven were used for dried fruits, onions, grains, and bread. He poured holy water, which he had gotten this morning at St. Nicholas Church, into a glass, a despondent Haba handed him large, hairy paintbrushes, which Haba Habinsky and Piotrek Petravskyi had picked up at the Heroiv Dnipra metro station, dipped them in the holy water and sprinkled it around.

The droplets flew far, all the way to the distant stands, passed them, and partially landed on the cookery display cases, lay there for a few seconds, and then got up and moved along. They circled near the transparent doors and went through them. Having flown outside, they paused for a moment, as if they were checking out Kyiv and thinking what should be done next, and then shot upward. Then, momentarily, in the glow of the lamp-posts, cars, and advertisement lights, a heavy, clear rain fell in a solid green wave over Kyiv.

"And, Vasyl, let our enemies fade,"[18] Peter said, sat next to Haba, accepted the bottle from him, glanced at the rain beyond the grey walls of the building, and also took a sip.

"Grant us victory, o Lord!" the plumber implored quietly, almost pathetically. "Let it be a small one, but one that is ours. And grant us peace in our land, light, harmony, and hope."

"And let my mother think of me, at least from time to time," Haba whispered and lowered his head, "because not one of us knows where it is that he or she shall perish."

"And Habinsky's mom, Holy Lord," Vasyl voiced sternly, "let her know that this dude loves her and thinks about her every day."

"And father," Habinsky quietly uttered and began to cry.

"And let Habinsky's father have good health, bread on the table and, at least occasionally, tranquility."

"He has issues with his memory, with his stomach, and with his heart. They are cold and frightened in city Z, but they, holy father, will never leave it."

"Grant our families a guardian angel, o Lord," ardently pleaded Vasyl, quieted for a moment, and then with prayer and holy water walked along the stands.

Sosipatra

Metamorphosis: 1) a quick transformation of form and structure, which is noticeable in insects; 2) the transformation of a personality.
—*Encyclopedia of Psychology*

Regarding Sosipatra, she had had no real love experience, even though she was only a few years younger than Haba. Lovers were present in her life, but they were like her. There even was a husband. That poor guy worked with her father at the coalmine. But those pitiful penetrations and un-beautiful and un-beneficial arousals, in which she participated between her sixteenth and her twenty-first springs—those thin hot sweats, impassionate kisses, imperfect cunnilingus, and insincere blow jobs—could not really be considered to be sex.

Sometimes people—not just in the Donbas, by the way—try to seem older by performing ridiculous exercises, most of which are copied from classic German porn (if you know what that means), or from manuals, which, before the war, were sold in Donetsk at the local Russian book market and were presented as "the Kama Sutra extended," the Indian erotic treatise written by the doctor Vātsyāyana who, it is widely known, was aroused by the sculptural representations of the Black Pagoda temple. Thus, first came architecture, and then—sex. And this is worth knowing. But be that as it may, there was no one over there in the Donbas, to be honest, that could keep the Indian traditions going—besides the staff and the freelance workers of the local publishing houses.

***

The office is quiet but stirring. It's been a week since the latest salvation was supposed to have gone to print but the Director looked over that junk that they had pasted together for him and gently, yet firmly, let it be known that they need to keep up with the trends.

"Understood," the Editor-in-Chief says, "so that is how they did it. But can you modify this pose to make it something that is novel? The Director is right, we cannot just duplicate things because that is a copyrights violation and, even if it is not a violation, then why the hell should we publish something that is already present in the market in one way or another? In other words, we need to keep working in this direction, work along the boundary of the well-known and the unknowable. We need a creative approach."

The Compiler looks at the figures of the Black Pagoda that light up his monitor. He ponders.

"Of course, we can add a guy here or, for instance, a pair here or there," he indicates with his finger on the monitor, "so that they'd do *this or that* with the girl. What do you think, will this fly?"

"*This or that*," the Chief repeats, "is what the head of the marketing department will do to us later."

"I got it, ok, but what, then, do you want me to do in this situation?"

"Hold up," the Chief nervously takes a sip of coffee, "well, why not this or that? It would be more in fashion with today's political and cultural trends."

"You think so?" the Complier says playing dumb.

"I am positive," the Chief says. "And later, increasing or decreasing the number of people simultaneously having sex, well, that's, how should I explain it, an easy path, I would say—an extensive one, but we are looking for something intensive, something completely new."

"And we'll add to the blow job breathing exercises, and a focus on the Svadhishthana and the Muladhara. It will come out completely authentic."

"Save that for your wife," the Editor says, "we should be focused not on chakras but on sales. And also, how can you focus on something, while giving someone a blow job?"

"I am not the one to ask," the Complier carefully gives notice.

He and the Chief silently stare at one another for some time.

"Aha," the Chief finally says, "I understand, you're not. But, dude, if this crap we are drawing doesn't sell well then the publishing house will cease working with you."

"God forbid," the Complier says wiping the sweat from his face. "What's up with your air conditioners? Such a hot spring and they're barely doing anything."

"Lena!" the Chief yells. "Get us some beers."

Lena brings two opened bottles. And it is with them that everything begins. After the third round, they ask Lena to stay, because the conversation has become quite animated, and it is precisely Lena who is particularly suited to contribute to such conversations. Around midnight, after the Chief has been delivered to the entrance of his building, Lena and the Compiler ride in a taxi, unreservedly talking about something absolutely magnificent, and then they suddenly begin making out.

At one o'clock, the not-so-young and very tired Compiler goes out on the balcony for some fresh air. Lena, of course, goes out there too, he looks at her young thighs, breasts, and butt, which sparkle in the light of the magical Donbas lampposts, and suddenly it becomes clear to him that he could indeed complete the work of Mr. Vātsyāyana. But he was not born in that century, not in that country, and not into that family. He married not that wife and not for that reason that is needed for that kind of work. And Lena, what about Lena. She would never marry him. Even if he were twenty years younger.

The Complier saddens and drinks cognac with lemon until morning, gradually sobering up. Lena sleeps like an angel and doesn't wake up when he closes the door behind him. Just don't bother her, I beg you, she needs her rest. See how she snores? In the evening, she is going on a date with her future husband.

And the morning streets, upon which the Compiler will head home, look on ironically and somewhat removed. The sky is not so much grey as not having been washed for a long time, perhaps three thousand years. He'll return home, open his mail, read a letter from his wife, who is vacationing with the kids at her parents in

Moscow. He'll take a cold shower. He'll go up to the fridge, drink a can of light beer and then down half a bottle of vodka, to go with his scrambled eggs. In bed, he'll wrap himself in a blanket and will dreadfully cry out loud for a long time, until a dream comes along.

***

That is why the enormity and, in the end, the enormous problem Habinsky had was that he, for better or for worse, was able to see in Sosipatra a remarkable feminine nature, geared toward a fully metaphysical approach to everything in the world, including to relations between the sexes. And this is not so easy to do within a collective of people of the female kin, who tend to gather by the walls of the university to escape the boredom of the city's cafés. And, just between us, he would be better off not doing this because—what kind of person has that kind of personality? What kind of creature is this? Is she just a part of him, or is he really only her breath. Did they both just imagine this? He could never know for sure.

Either way, Haba was grading students' papers in a storeroom one spring when she stopped by there for some reason. And here, before us, like before curious scholars of culture, rises the issue of the typical storeroom, and of the laboratory room, in the everyday sexual lives of the Eastern Slavs.

But first it is important to comprehend what spring is like in the Donbas, more specifically—in city Z. It is beauty absolute. And, first of all, it's the apricot, the queen of all the fruit-bearing trees of eastern Ukraine, which strides through large cities and small villages in springtime days and floods the Universe all the way up to Orion's belt with a froth that is both bitter and sweet. From farmsteads and city streets, the apricot dives into forest patches, circles above the shores of the ponds, sets up its guard on both sides of paths, peeps into every window, dissolves in the lungs and the eyes of both the old and the young, becoming their breath and their faith.

Secondly, obviously, it's the coal, the chemical industry, and metallurgy, which do their difficult and necessary job, adding a flavor of death and hopelessness to the apricot's aroma. It is only during springtime that the pollution doesn't elicit true hate in the people and that it is, instead, accepted as a completely organic addition to this celebration of nature's rebirth. Because it—nature, of course—is as dead as it is alive. And it is dead and alive at the same time. Just like Ukraine, of course, or, let's say, you, my immortal reader, or that girl who once answered to the name Sosipatra.

Oh, those lips, those thighs, those big and cool, size-twelve feet. Like those of a small giant. Oh, how uninhibitedly and effortlessly she took off her clothes! Oh, the clumsiness of those kisses, the beautifully bad taste of her jewelry. All this happiness entered Habinsky's life when the sun began to set in the steppe, and when the steppe finally conquered the city and began shooting icy and playful streams of ancient sadness into it. April, more accurately, the very beginning of May, of year such-and-such AD forever and ever entered Haba's life and transformed him into someone else.

***

Sosipatra had actually attracted Habinsky's attention earlier, but in a completely different manner. First of all, she was small, like an insect. Second, she was unbearably funny. Her clothes, her makeup, her smile, and her movements were all funny. A pretty, even beautiful, girl, svelte, decent, but why so funny, damn it, Haba would think every time he saw her. Third, it was her voice. It was doll-like, as if phony. But, at the same time, not repulsive. Just weirdly funny. It seemed like the Creator, when he was bringing his plans for her to fruition, could not decide what he really wanted in the end: a large doll that is happy and funny, or a person who is funny but, simultaneously, absolutely tragic. She was marked by essential exaggeration, an incompatibility between form and her own sense.

After laughter, for every normal creature of the masculine gender, of course, would come wonder. And it was after it—that complex stage of critical thinking—that Sosipatra's doll-like nature began to elicit in Haba some sort of subconscious, uncontrollable horror that was, in some strange manner, connected with a desire to take control of it, this horror.

Every time he would see Sosipatra in the university corridors, he would attempt to hide, to disappear, to get out of the way of the trajectory of her movement, because when she, Sosipatra, would see Haba, she would always come up with a reason to walk up to him, to ask about something, and to chat. He was successful in doing this for some time: he was not a full-time instructor, he would only be there to teach his own elective courses and, obviously, would only visit the department when it was necessary. But over time, Sosipatra had memorized the schedule of his lectures and of his office hours, as well as the simple layout of the building, so he really had no chance.

"Habriel Bohdanovych," Sosipatra would address Haba with his patronymic at just that moment when he thought he was in the clear. "I am here waiting for you."

"O Sosipatra! Such a pleasure!" Haba would place his leather briefcase on the windowsill and look at his watch. No matter what you do there are still a few minutes left before his lesson. There is no chance of avoiding a conversation.

"I read that book that you recommended to me last time," she says in such a voice and with such a facial expression that Haba instinctively begins to get the chills, "It is so interesting! Sooo interesting!"

"You like it?"

"Certainly!" she unknowingly begins, as she always does, to bop up and down, which looks quite comical in her case. Haba can feel how from far, far away spasms of laughter approach full speed ahead. They're unbearable, shameless, and probably borne out of the anger of existence and not of happiness. "Dostoevsky's idiot is so nice, very much so, but he, like all Russians in general, has a few screws loose."

"I would say that this is a contradictive thesis, we cannot allow ourselves to speak about all Russians in such a manner..."

"You know what," she interrupts him, "when I was a kid, they would call me Shevchenko."

In boxing, this is known as an uppercut. Habinsky immediately becomes red and begins to bite his lip, almost piercing it.

"You—Shevchenko? Why Shevchenko?" His breathing overwhelms him and uncontrollable tears well up in his eyes.

"I don't even remember," Sosipatra nods, ponders, forms a star with her lips and finally turns into a doll, "maybe because I was the only one in class that had read his *Kobzar*, or maybe because I look like him."

"Like who?"

"Like Shevchenko," the girl looks sadly and begins to rock side to side, again nods her head, "He was very cute when he was young," and quickly adds, "by the way, I wanted to ask you something."

"Ask away."

"Habriel Bohdanovych, do you have a wife?"

"I don't." But he cannot take this anymore. "Ok, Sosipatra, it was very nice to see you, but I've got a lesson to go to."

"You promised to recommend a book," the doll says, bouncing up and down a couple of times.

This is so funny that it merits a killing, Haba reddens like a poppy and, unconsciously and without bustle, begins to pray (*God have mercy on me, God have mercy on me*).

"Well, I have a husband whom I don't love and whom I fear," she continues.

"Why do you fear him?" Haba inquires in a completely mechanical manner, because he needs to quash the great Homeric laugh that is ready to burst out of his lungs and roll down in boulders along the half-empty floors of the department.

"How should I put it," she muses. "I don't really fear him, it's more like I feel bad for him. He's hairy, messy, nasty, and doesn't read books," Sosipatra replies slowly, extending the vowels comically. "You see, it turns out that I got married very young, I didn't know what I was doing. Even now I can't recall how that happened. Does that ever occur to you?"

"Habriel," a linguist colleague from the Department of General Linguistics takes Habinsky by the elbow, "can I talk to you for couple of minutes?"

"Yes!" Haba says with incredible readiness, "You'll have to excuse me, Sosipatra, I need to take care of something!"

"Ok," the girl simultaneously raises her eyebrows and lines up her feet one behind the other, "but what about the book?"

"Read Andersen's tales, you'll like them," Habinsky says, grabs Ferdinand de Saussure by the elbow and takes off with him to the faculty office. At the office, empty and full of the street noise coming in through the open window, he begins to laugh. At length, frighteningly, and to the point of tears. Saussure looks at him with a detached scholarly interest, lights up a cigarette and goes up to the window. He smokes, smiles, and watches as Habinsky twists and clutches at his sides, dying from laughter. After a minute, his fit passes. Haba settles down, wipes his tears, shakes his head. A heavy sorrow begins to pour into his lungs, his temples tremble, a yawn erupts.

"You'll have to excuse me," he says covering his mouth with his hand, "It's a nervous reaction. Happens every now and then."

"It happens to all of us," Ferdinand comments carefully.

Back at home after eight, Habinsky makes himself dinner and thinks about Sosipatra. He floats the idea that this repulsive creature is perhaps the most interesting thing to have taken place in his life in the past few years. The next day he will sit down to work in the storeroom, having gotten the keys to it from Ferdinand. The sun begins to set over the horizon, rain is on the way, a bitter, happy yet sad scent will pour into the window. Who knows how Sosipatra found out where Habinsky usually reviews the students' reports. Perhaps she has known this all along.

***

Some time, not much at all, passes and he says, "Sosi, you are the comical repulsion of my life."

"I know," the little, comical creature bounces, shakes her breasts, kisses his lips, arms, and shoulders, and then hastily runs to take a shower. Because she has a class. It's morning. In the evening, everything is different.

"You are amazing," he says in the evening, "my Patra," he joyfully laughs, washing her with a sponge: little knees and thighs; ears that are a bit hairy, funny and too big for such a miniature girl; a large nose with a little bump; wonderful, quiet breasts, which open up in his palms, like buds (of course) of a rose and the blossoms (surely) of a birch; and everything that he finds between her legs.

"O Patra, my partridge,"[1] he would say and sink into a collapsed Soviet sofa overfilled with the smells of tobacco and coffee, feeling the back of the girl's head, which had the scent of buckwheat honey and cheap Chinese shampoo, bobbing beneath his hands.

The sofa and everything that they did on it on those first few days are just the funny beginning of an irreversible path. Funny, quiet, and clumsy, like a child who has just begun learning how to walk, or like a young war that has just taken its first steps and is not sure of itself yet. But, in a couple of weeks, it will learn things that the Compiler of the manual for the Russian-language champions of the Kama Sutra would never be able demonstrate (*because Lena is not the kind of woman who would allow this to happen, she will soon get married (already is married). And who knows why, by the way. And then, after the war begins (it has begun and continues to take place), her husband will join "the rebels" (the money is not great, but money is money), somehow, one evening she'll think of the Complier. His sad, grey eyes, a funny habit of asking her every time whether she had come or not, his death (in the past, in the future). Somewhere, not far from the city center, after the pro-Ukrainian march in the spring of 2014, he will be severely beaten by young guys in balaclavas. He is able to get home on his own, but he only lives for another week. For Lena, the only thing left of the Compiler are memories and the manual, which he was able to complete just before the start of the war. It is evening. It's quiet, but, at the same time, shooting can be heard somewhere outside the city. She flips through sketches demonstrating sexual partners in various positions. She reads and weeps. It's a valuable thing—the Kama Sutra in a time of war*), movie actresses never think about such things, and they cannot even be imagined by female students of this blessed university. Haba, grey and exhausted by life, delved into the world of quiet caresses, endless idiotic laughter, comical tenderness, and unconditional doom, that fluttered ahead so clearly and so directly, like blue kid-sized underpants and huge (compared to the

underpants) yellow socks belonging to Sosipatra. There
are things in life that are capable of producing both tears
and laughter.

***

But first there was the laboratory—to be more specific,
the storeroom. A large table that still remembers the
death of Stalin. Faded wallpaper which seems to have
been glued to these walls way back during the cold summer of fifty-three. A pile of folders full of documents are
stacked up against the wall. Time suspended in papers.
Old and useless term papers and reports written by people who no longer remember their *alma mater*. For whom
was all this written? Why? Millions of wasted moments,
squandered expectations, and youth magnificently
turned to dust.[2]

Unsold copies of textbooks, which had been produced
for many years by lecturers from various humanities departments: *The Poetical Achievements of Heinrich III's Min-
ions*, *Towards the Question of Adjectives at Slavic Weddings*,
*The Problems of Language Studies and Industrial Production
in the Upper Volga Region*, *Coarse Pronouns in Voroshylovhrad*,
Do the Oxen Bellow as a Hamletian Question, and *Tychyna as
Tiutchev*.

In the closet, mugs, plates, tin soldiers, corks, porce-
lain ballerinas, and bronze busts of Ferdinand de Saussure
and Baudouin de Courtenay jingle amongst themselves.
The latter two discuss the departmental booze-fest that
took place here last week. It smells of dust, paper, cheap
coffee, the remnants of a hot dog lunch, cheap tobacco,
the wet asphalt of University Street, traffic, the grey rainy

sky, in which the sun occasionally makes an appearance, and linden trees, which have been observing university life for five decades in a row.

Around 5 pm she gently cracked open the door to the storeroom and stuck her head in through the gap. She saw Haba, who was reading something. She contentedly smiled, pulled herself out of the room, looked around the empty corridor, again stuck her face into the storeroom and thought it over. Then, she opened the door wider and entered. Having closed the door behind her, she again paused to think for a moment. Then, she locked the door using a big hook marked with green paint and, in an instant, stood in front of Habinsky.

"Good evening, Habriel Bohdanovych," she said, somewhat sorrowfully, "So, here I am. There you have it."

Habinsky slowly lifted his eyes. The figure by the door was not a human figure. The figure that looked at him had never belonged to the sapiens sapiens species. It was something different. But, its small height notwithstanding, it was something that was great and powerful. Something that caused Habinsky's skin to be covered in chills, or maybe sweat.

"Who are you?" he asked, unaware of what he was saying, he reddened and wanted to rectify himself, but the girl was not at all offended.

"Oh," she jumped up, "don't be silly! It's me, Sosipatra, the student of the so-and-so faculty of Stus University.[3] I read Andersen—not a bad writer, but horrifying, muddled, and sad. I was given his books to read as a kid. Everything that takes place there is scary and confusing." She fell silent, curtsied for some reason and, without being invited, sat on a pile of folders in the corner by the closet. "On the other hand, he did write for children. And that is what kids need."

"How so?" Haba became interested.

"You need to keep frightening them until something becomes of them," Sosipatra explained. "How about I make you some coffee?"

"Coffee?" Haba glanced at the window which aggressively carried in the smells of apricot flowers and the smell of the factory. The sun appeared from behind the clouds like a large metallurgical *Prunus armeniaca*. One wanted to grab it and squeeze out its yellow juice and pulp, so that it would stream along the streets and hills of the city, flood the rivers and ponds, and then harden, thick and yellow, upon the freshly-green outfit that is May. Habinsky got up and closed the window.

"I wanna do it!" the creature ran to the tea kettle, checked on the water level, turned it on, hopped up and down a few times, and smiled.

Habinsky sat down on the old, squashed couch, which smelled either of fleas or cognac, and lit up a smoke.

"Today, Mr. Habriel, I frantically ran through a bunch of stores," Sosipatra shared and scrunched her ears, "it's called 'shopping'. Did you know that?" She swung her hips right and left three times and looked at Haba to see whether he had noticed her routine and, determining that he hadn't, briefly yawned. "I don't like being in school in the springtime. Do you like my pantyhose?" She put some coffee and sugar in a cup, turned towards Haba and lifted her skirt. Habinsky quietly checked out her slender legs, her crazy, tiny pupils, her charming, funny, and unbelievably attractive face (*comical and beautiful—categories that are incompatible, but not in this case*). She stood like that with her skirt lifted for no less than one minute, looking into Habinsky's eyes.

"You can let it down now," he finally said, "I got to see everything."

"And what do you think?" the skirt slowly lowered itself. "They cost me X-amount of money. Do you know why I bought them?"

"Why?"

"I wanted you to like me. Do you like me?" Sosipatra put her arms to her sides and spun around. "You see how small I am, you see? Pretty nice, right? And this is where my stomach is, it's small, but it's there. It has the scent of ginger and of the sun. Can you see?"

"I can," Habinsky laughed, his blood hitting his temples so hard he could barely hear anything.

"I have such beautiful breasts. Can I show them to you?"

"Sosipatra," Habinsky slowly moved his rubber, frozen lips, "you are a married woman. And I am your instructor."

"Yes! That's right! Everything is lining up perfectly. I think about that all the time."

"What is so perfect about it?"

"You live near the university, I could come visit you every morning, afternoon, every evening, if you'd let me. That would be fun, wouldn't it? You would give me books to read, and I'd read them, getting wiser by the minute. But now—coffee!" (*The teapot with a banged-up spout splatters boiling water, the smell of coffee, rays hit the ceiling—the sun of the Donbas apricot sets down behind the inevitably European horizon.*)

Haba got up and walked up to Sosipatra, put his palms on her head and slowly lowered them onto her shoulders.

He felt the warmth of the little brain, the softness of to-day's lavish hairdo, and the scent of cheap perfume. The girl stood numbly, except for her trembling hands. He pulled her up against his body, felt the yearning hot body and, simultaneously, an incredible tenderness. Tears, like ichor, left his eyes in a quiet pain, and flowed along his unshaven cheeks.

"Kiss me on the back of my neck, Mr. Habriel, or else I'm going to start hiccupping," she pitifully pleaded. "I sometimes get a nervous reaction."

"It happens to all of us," Haba carefully kissed the pink doll. Very carefully, as if she were capable of melting and leaving behind her a trace of bitter, bright-yellow, apricot laughter.

***

Sosipatra grew up in an ordinary family. Her father was a coalminer and a communist. Her mother worked as a secretary at the regional branch of the people's education institute. It is through these connections that the girl got into college. Sosipatra's husband was a huge, quiet man and generally a good guy. After every shift, he drank vodka with his buddies. After last year's accident at the coal mines, he lost his sexual mojo and developed a habit of deliberately inflicting pain in bed (*the mine face collapsed, he spent three and a half days in solitude*). She would scream at half volume so that her parents, who are watching TV on the other side of the wall, wouldn't hear, while he laughed (*because his heart cried*). Nowadays, to be clear, he doesn't need any other kind of sex except this kind, he only needs Sosipatra to whisperingly scream and cry (*she's alive, this wife of his, this immediately becomes obvious*). For who else is there to blame for everything in this country? Children, women, and the elderly. In the morning, he would show remorse, beg forgiveness, and then go to work.

Everything else was just like it was for everybody else, nothing special. Dim, everyday life. Toxic smoke from the chimneys and slag heaps. The cries of roosters, the screams of pigs, puddles and mud. Kids going to school. They lived far away in a village that may become a suburb of the city in three to four decades (*that is, of course, if the Donbas returns to Ukraine*). Thus, Sosi often chose to spend the night with her girlfriends in the dormitory and the family got used to that.

During rainy evenings this spring, when the sky was ablaze with red and pink swastikas that burned above city Z, she and Haba would play various games. Later, a heavy, dark-green rain would fall in a heap on a city that had been aroused by spring. Sosipatra would lean against Haba and fall asleep. At night, the rains would grow stronger, the thunderclaps would become more dangerous than the morning news and his lover, like a swaddled infant, would tightly wrap herself into him, slowly peeling his skin off and swathing it onto herself. Naturally, he was larger than her, so his skin would be more than enough for Sosipatra to maintain her warmth. But, in the morning, the scholar would be left without any skin. He would end up being more naked than he was at birth: nothing but joints, muscles, and bones, and indefinite remains of internal culturological fat.

"What have you done to me," he would say quietly, placing his coffee on a little table by his bed. "I don't have any more skin. How am I gonna leave the house?"

She would wake up, laugh, work through his muscle fibers with her long fingers, drink coffee, leave cookie crumbs, hop, and jump. She would leave the door open when she'd use the toilet. She wanted him to look at her while she was peeing. Having peed to her heart's content, she would head off for classes at the university. Sosipatra was not a woman in the strict sense of the word. She couldn't be, she didn't know how to be, she wasn't born to be that. She was born for something else (*even less so to be a Donbas woman*). And she was aware of this and, perhaps, that's why she never complained about life. For those like her, life's never easy.

Having led the pink doll to the door, Haba would finally toss on a shirt, jump into his pants, put on socks and a tie, and cover his head with a hat, hiding the absolute lack of a scalp. He would stare at the green and black puddles and at the white flowers that had been smacked by the wind and the heavy night water, and would run off to his university department.

For some reason, he didn't feel like seeing his colleagues and, luckily, in his department, only the deaf and blind worked. They would not see his nakedness, his skinlessness, and his defenselessness. They would talk amongst themselves. They were busy with the end of the semester, with exams in literature, comparative linguistics, and culturology, with final reports, and with the defenses of theses, which, in August, will become the dust and ashes of college life. Only the old granny security guard, Halia, would make the sign of the cross every time

she would see Haba, when he would occasionally go out
to get some air, tobacco, and frankfurters, that is—hot
dogs. In May, they are particularly beneficial to those who
lecture in aesthetics, who always lack sleep, who don't
form skin in time, and thus slowly die, turn to glass and
fly away accompanied by a dry, quiet bell, to lands where
those, such as he, are awaited by an aesthetically uncom-
promising paradise of glass, two-story buildings, by air
filled with aloe, ambrosia, by the winds of shoreline cliffs,
by black tea, and bitter-salty rain.

Of course, in a few months, fresh news arrived in the
suburbs. Habinsky had not known anything about it. She
had simply stopped going to the university for a week.
And later, she returned to Haba, took off her clothes—and
he noticed. The little doll laughed when she spoke about
it and it is precisely then that Haba thought, for the first
time, that one day he'd have to kill that nice dude from
the suburbs, for that matter, a wonderful family man,
a supporter of forced pain.

By the way, this did not recur, there were no longer dark brown and red traces on her body, nor tales of
beatings. But something was taking place in that suburb, something that Sosipatra shielded Habinsky away
from. And the more she would shield him, the funnier
her life became. Haba would force himself to ask her
about what's going on, but she would never tell him the
truth. And the worst of it was that, in the depth of his
soul, he didn't want to know, because what could he really do about it even if he wanted to? That's why, for that
whole year before the war when they were together, Haba
avoided thinking about what their relationship may have
meant for her. That's why Habinsky didn't notice when

Sosipatra began transforming into a dragonfly, that is, into a typical Ukrainian Odonata.

***

In fact, for the past ten years, Habinsky avoided any news, good or bad (*to escape thoughts about Sosipatra's life in the suburbs*). He hadn't watched television the past fifteen years, didn't read any newspapers, even less so the local ones. A well-planned strategy of living a hermetic life helped him to survive in the world.

He learned how to not think about his relationship with his parents which, in the year before the war, was akin to the warm relations between Luther and the Catholic Church. To not know is, sometimes, the only way to not worry, to not be tortured by pity and longing, to not scream in your sleep, to not slowly drink vodka for days, to not reach for the gas valve, the knife blade, to not prick the pupils of the conscious with motley and insatiable branches of family space, that, with every one of its touches, creates the impossibility of seeing, breathing, and understanding. That much was clear.

And not-knowing, and simultaneously understanding that you really don't know (*maybe the two of them beat Sosipatra together, her husband and her own father, beating her so as not to leave any traces*), and having a precise, authorized by a higher organ *Canon of Not-knowing*, that has been perfected and almost begged to fruition—that is true art. And Habinsky has been developing this forever. And, in that sense, he has reached certain zeniths. In 2014, he was perhaps the only person in the city for whom the latest news was the countries of Europe forming the European Union.

The catechism of blessed ignorance emerged slowly in his life. During childhood, you had to not know everything that you knew about those people who surrounded you. Because, firstly, they each had their own *Canon of Not-knowing* and, secondly, they were good people who knew not what they were doing. You had to not know about your country and city, about your male and female friends, about women and men, about their kids and desires, about light and darkness, mom and dad, brothers and sisters, about grandmother, grandfather and granduncle, about their past, and about your own future.

The fate of your grandfather and his brother on your mother's side of the family—that is something that in Soviet times, and, honestly after those times, too, needed not to be known. The father and mother of his grandfather—Oleksii Iehorovych, and, respectively, of his granduncle—Ivan Iehorovych, were shot to death in the beginning of the 1920s by the Bolsheviks in front of their children, when the older child had just turned six.

***

Only occasionally, in his dreams, would Haba see the large, picturesque village Kushchi, in which his ancestors had lived their entire lives, in which they had a sizeable homestead—a mill and barns, a venerable two-story home, a small piano (*a collection of several decades-worth of European academic journals, ancient folios from an enormous library, bronze chandeliers, furniture from Warsaw, neckties from Paris, stallions raised by great-grandpa and purchased by*

Germans and Turks). Those dreams would always include the month of February, heavy and too-large-for-such-small-and-loved-children, with its sky that burned (*like a Christmas tree glass ball*) with its cold and blue darkness.

The dream would always begin with the sad and stern faces of the villagers, who were rallied at this two-story farmstead of these well-to-do villagers by early afternoon (*in the dream, Haba would always ponder why his great-grandpa and great-grandma hadn't left the country*). People should be able to see what could happen to enemies of the Soviet state (*well, not really enemies— great-grandpa's brother became an admiral in the Soviet navy*).

But the shootings didn't begin until 4 pm, by which time all their possessions would have been seized and loaded on to wagons that stretched in a long line all the way to the *kolhosp* office building.[4] By that time, everybody would be bitterly cold and would quietly curse the well-to do villagers, the Bolsheviks, the winter, and the month of February. The frost, as it turned out, was not too bad, but the snow would crackle as if large, black hares gnawed at the anthracite below the boots of the Bolsheviks. Rods of smoke from stacks would rhthmically twist into the low, dark-greyish sky. They would twist in and out. The smoke wouldn't go anywhere, it would flutter between the sky and the ground in grey-black tornados, painting winter's details, and refining the general rhythm of the dream.

Giant crows would scream. Kazimir the Universal would make large circles around the estate. The pulsating rhythm of the Kyiv metro would arrive at the site of the action in dark, warm waves, but there was no place for it to come from in 1922 AD, seven hundred miles from

that ravine, Khreshchatyi Iar. Wind gusts would bring
the smells of McDonald's and of the nearby deep Dnipro River.

The family was finally taken away from their homestead. The children were taken away from their parents
and stood around an ancient poplar tree that grew about
twenty yards from the building, just past a green fence.
The parents stood side by side against the western wall.

Great-grandpa Iehor stood quietly and stared straight
ahead of himself. He supported his wife by her left elbow. Great-grandma Oleksandra, who had lost her mind
during yesterday's interrogations (*they were asking her
about gold and jewelry*), quietly smiled, no longer feeling
any apprehension about the children being left alone in
the world, or any happiness that life was finally coming
to an end. Both stood barefoot on the snow, but they
couldn't, of course, feel the cold.

They had five little kids. The oldest, Lida, had turned
six in May (*in the 1950s she will end up in the Far East and
will become a mother in a large Ukrainian-Korean family*). The
twins Mariana and Lesia are five (*the former will disappear
after the Great Migration of Children to Kyiv, the latter will sell
silver and gold in Romania, will move to the States in the 1990s,
where traces of her disappear*). The two brothers—Oleksii
and Ivan (*they'll remain together up to their deaths, Ivan just
couldn't be separated from his brother, just as his fate couldn't
be untwined from that of his brother*)—stood a bit apart.
The three-year-old Ivan held on to Oleksii and no longer
cried, quietly whimpering instead (*having peed himself
several times out of fright, he smelled of urine and of sweet children's puke*). Oleksii wanted to bellow so badly, but he was
afraid of frightening his younger brother even more and

restrained himself, and when they began shooting the parents, he bit his left hand (*damaging his vein, the hand would hurt, especially in cold weather, until the day he died*) to refrain from screaming.

After a few days, it is the neighbors who will toss the stiff and burnt corpses into the wagon and take them away. They will tie heavy rocks to the bodies and dump them into the river, through a rectangular hole in the ice by the left bank, where, in the unfathomable depths, catfish live and the people's truth sleeps (*for millions of years, cold, greenish branches of ancient willows hover over that hole*).

After the frozen crowd was told a few zealous revolutionary words, they were allowed to disperse. People would scatter to their houses without looking at the kids, who remained standing by the fence. Those who were the last to leave, drunk on vodka and on the feeling of holy impunity, torched the homestead from all four sides.

The wind picked up, Kazimir yelled for the final time and flew west, nighttime was arriving, the many building additions lit up, and a black smoke set off circling around the short hills above the road and the field and above the frozen river and the steppe, which began just past the forests of Quiet Sloboda—the three or four homes of a large German family, half-ruined back in 1918 (*in 1922, Markus the Pilgrim died in one of them*).

And it is at this moment that the tragedy would always end.

Everything would harden for a moment and then the dead and bloody great-grandpa and great-grandma would get up from where they were lying (*that is how Gertrude, Antigone, Hamlet, Polynices, Eteocles, Claudius, and Laertes usually do it after the end of the fifth act*). They would go up to the children and embrace them. The children would be happy with the change in the situation and would not really be baffled by it (*in reality, they had hoped that everything that is evil and horrific would end up being a dream*). Blood would slowly drip down great-grandma Oleksandra's forehead, but this would not make her less attractive. Her smiling face would radiate a joyful, warm, clean, and cognitive insanity. In a few minutes, the villagers would begin returning, the downtrodden and the poor, with their flags and banners, tired of the winter. Among the latest to arrive would be the drunk, embarrassed commissars. An empty wagon, tied to an old horse named Aleko,[5] would arrive last. No one would be driving it, so the horse would only return to the dream if called to do so by a spirit.

Everyone would congratulate everyone else for their victory, they would kiss, sincerely show remorse towards those that were shot, and the latter would forgive them, and would also apologize for some old misunderstandings. Great-grandpa Iehor would happily lift the three-year old Ivan in his arms and would begin dancing a brisk, yet melancholic, dance with him. Oleksandra would look at them and smile.

The blue snow would fall in large puffy clumps that looked just like the cotton candy that Haba would buy Sosipatra by the carousel in the city park. The sky would turn black and gold. It looked like someone was changing the decorations before a new show. Oboes and French horns would intermittently sound in the orchestra pit of being. Sometimes somebody would laugh or cough. The first violin would occasionally play a few high notes and then stop, once again play, and then interrupt the singing. However, there were no listeners to be seen. Nor musicians, for that matter.

The oboes and French horns would agree on something and an overture would begin. Its sound would be soft but also very distressed. It would summon and promise something that was beyond the margins of this stage (*beyond the margins of the 1920s*). Habinsky's mother and father would finally exit the burning home (*they were born a whole epoch after these events and never knew about, or never wanted to know about, this execution*). Next to them old grandpa Ivan (*to the left of father, carrying a gramophone*) and grandpa Oleksii (*to the right of father, carrying a few records*) would walk. Old, grey, and long since dead Oleksii would smile at himself, at a young version of himself that was in his mother's arms, who herself looked three times younger than him.

"So that's basically how it happened," grandpa would say, patting Habinsky's dad on the shoulder. "And, throughout your life, you, my son, kept saying 'the Party,' 'Communism.' But that's really how it was, boy, in my life, just that kind of party and that kind of communism."

"But I didn't know, dear Oleksii Iehorovych," father would shrug his shoulders. "If I had known, I would have never had, I wouldn't have..."

"I understand, dear," grandpa would tenderly smile.

"Well, it's your fault, because you never mentioned this at all."

"If you knew about all of this in the 1970s, how would you have survived later?" grandpa Oleksii would ask.

"How would any of us have survived?" mother would add.

A thicker snow would pour down. Heavy drums would be added to the violins and the oboes (*straining their tiny souls*). Habinsky's father couldn't take it anymore and would yell into the orchestra pit: stop it, please, this is torture. At first the oboes, then the violins and the French horns, and then after them the drums, all would quiet. The musicians would cough and converse frustratingly. But, perhaps, they understood that it is better not to argue with Habinsky's father. Smiling to the public, Oleksii Iehorovych would switch on the gramophone, Ivan Iehorovych would throw on a record. And, finally, Mahalia Jackson would begin singing "I'm on My Way."

As she sang, Haba would pull back from these people, from the village Kushchi, from the '20s decade of some inexplicable century—one of the endless and bloody centuries that his fatherland lived through—from his parents and their parents, and from the latter's parents as well. From the blue sky and the burning-yellow ashes. From the never-ending horrible winter and vanilla snow, which took on a bit of an ivory shade in those places splattered with fresh human blood.

He would awake from coldness and sadness. It would be dark beyond the window. Half past three. His face heavier from tears, his head—from pain. Breathing with difficulty, he would get up and go to the bathroom. He'd drink water, look into the mirror and see Hermes Trismegistus.

Keep in mind, you trivial and miserable person, in life's tough times you can only really depend on your own reflection in the mirror—a twin with cinnamon eyes. Full of energy or sick, drunk, happy, joyous, young, old, wise, idiotic, or painfully sober—*he who does not exist*—he is always with you. He who cannot be known, and not because it is forbidden, but simply because he does not exist when you are on your own, because only an Other can see us. *I'm on my way to Canaan Land, I'm on my way, oh, to Canaan Land, On my way to Canaan Land, On my way, glory hallelujah, I'm on my way.*

***

Maybe it was precisely when the proffesor-president[6] (*a subspecies of the wise professor*) unexpectedly and permanently left for Russia that Haba got bronchitis for the second time in a year. That notwithstanding, he worked a lot: he taught in three different departments at a time and did extra work as a tutor on weekends. He would run around the city like crazy, capturing with his mouth the wintery breath of the days, that were grey as village mice, and he'd always count his money to see if he had enough to take his little girl on a trip somewhere in August, or, let's say, in September, for at least a week (*the plans of a person who does not desire to know anything*). If, of course, those glorious days ever do arrive.

February was coming to an end, March was beginning, the war approached, it was the beginning of the last spring of the old life. Haba checked his temperature, he felt like he was dying. At times, at the edge of his consciousness, he accepted the thoughts of his colleagues that America is starting a war with Russia in Ukraine, that the Masons of the European Union have gone insane, that the time for change had come and that God forbid we should live during such a time, but it does look like He allowed it to come.

Habinsky saw rallies gathering by the regional administration building, stopped by there a few times, listened
a bit (*which would make him zone out*), and then kept going. The city was changing so rapidly that there was no
way of keeping up with its transformation. Such a great
distance between today and tomorrow was unfolding
that one could not traverse it even in one of Leonardo da
Vinci's helicopters. The process had gathered such speed
that, one time, Habinsky was afraid of not recognizing
himself, of moving into forgetfulness where there are no
means of orientation.

By that time, he could not envision his life without her.
Without his Sosi. The funny, long-harried Patra. Without
the doll, which he would enter, crawl about, fly into, fall
into like into insanity, sink into like into melancholy, or
plunge into like into childhood. Only because of her was
he studying Latin, doing laundry, writing poems, feed-
ing birds, and singing spiritual hymns. He would pray
for her in temples of various religions and buy her toys
and lingerie. In conscious dreams, he would die the hair
on his head and his grey hairy balls in the light colors of
a future October, because Sosipatra loved October and
Calvados. Utilizing samokysh,[7] black currants, strawber-
ries, church candles, and Saturday litanies, he prepared
yogurts, cunnilingus, and lessons in the philosophy of
art. Heqet herself taught him how to play a solo on that
shamisen of vast and endless male solitude.[8]

But the war had already begun. A war between non-existence and existence. And, in the end, the transformation of the city reached Sosipatra as well. Her mother died
suddenly at the start of February. And a month later, her
father and husband left the coalmines and occupied the

regional administration building, together with other weird people. The girl suddenly tasted a freedom she had never felt before and a will she had never asked for. And, naturally, by March, Sosipatra began finding new lovers. And why not? Because between the Funny and the Grand there is, honestly, just an F sharp of difference. And, at that, her husband (*Haba saw him a couple of times: stocky, wide, with constant booze-breath and a red-yellow, surprisingly stylish, cap on his head*) began looking at her "excursions" absolutely leniently (*for some reason, this interested Haba the most out of everything that was taking place so quickly in city life*).

Now, from the perspective of an Obolon space and time, Haba saw that Sosipatra had simply fallen in love with the blue and black air of the new times, with the black wave of total changes, and that is why she rejected any discussions about moving (*please, stop, she would comically purse her lips and laugh*).

Yes-yes, Haba would say to himself, yes-yes, it is impossible to preserve anything. In May, he had conversations with Sosipatra almost every day, in which, every time, he came to understand that the doll would never abandon her city. And Habinsky's parents did not want to leave the city either (*"you are reasoning like a non-Russian"*).[9]

It's strange, but, for some reason, this kept happening to Habinsky rather often. People who had never met—or even heard about each other—felt and said the same exact things when they were in his presence. It is as if, through them, someone completely different was speaking to him.

***

In his diary, Haba wrote: "After a certain time, her hunting begins to take place in the evenings. She eats butterflies, actors from the city theater, average businessmen, maybugs conserved in their own juice, large and small bees, house flies and horse flies, philologists, and pro-Russian male praying mantises. All the while continuing to live with me, although I am sure she had been proposed other arrangements. And she would nonetheless return to me almost every day. But why? For what reason? She comes at night and quietly lies down to sleep. In the morning, she barely touches her food, washes it down with coffee, smokes, smiles, and says nothing. Then we have sex, because it is during the daytime that Sosipatra prefers to demonstrate the behavior associated with multiplication.

Long, green wings with a dense web of veins appeared on her. Short, barely-visible whiskers. Her eyes were now made up of tens of thousands of facets. The upper windows of her soul determine the form of her body, the lower—the colors. She only pairs up with me in the air. Her arms have strengthened and have become like large, strange, black additions to an entirely insect-like body."

She would catch Haba in the air, hold him in front of her, circle between the kitchen and a large window, which opened up to an old, Soviet-style courtyard and would slowly bring him into her large, greedy vagina. Only his arms, head, and a part of his chest would be free. Haba didn't really like this very much, but he truly had no choice, if you know what I mean. He would rock back and forth in the warm, damp bush and would think about the pricelessness of basic natural relations that are not obscured by metamorphoses that take place in life during wartime.

The sounds of normal life, which, at first glance, were not about horrific and decisive transformations, would flow in through a little ventilation window—but this was just an illusion. Haba would consistently feel that the situation was worse outside his window than it was on his side of the window. At least his arms and head remained free. Which could not be said about city Z as a live urban organism. Together with his lover, it was transforming into something else.

Strange people, strange conversations. A wind of fear, misunderstanding, and despair would tumble in waves from the center of the city to its peripheries and would return a hundred times stronger. The earth beneath one's feet would shift and sway, smack in the middle of the day. And during the night, the long and restless night, entire neighborhoods would disappear and, in the early morning, completely new ones would take their place, unprecedented ones, settled by other sorts of creatures. Sometimes, the old ones would return while the new ones wouldn't go anywhere. In March 2014, two or three different variations of names co-existed for the same streets in the coal mining districts. They would argue among themselves, stratify, push one another into oblivion, mutually destroy themselves, unite, and lead an endless war.

From these transformations, somewhere in the depths of the brain, a long, penetrating sound would appear, tremble, and fall, forcing the eyes to exude not tears but the green water of a future total forgetting. In the dreams of these days, countless monochromatic creatures would appear that conducted long conversations beyond the boundaries of the main plot, they would push him, laugh, pull Haba by the ears, by his hair, twist his fingers, slide into his mouth with clumsy ideas, and loosen his teeth.

Strangely, these dreams would usually be warm and peaceful. Haba would run along the streets of his childhood with its short, yellow and light-green buildings, and warm his face with the miniature fiery-dark sun. He would part with the dry, yellow pollen of his local fatherland, with the sunny wind of his childhood, with the rotating eternal tornados on both sides of the narrow roads, with the women and their big sad eyes.

After the warm dreams, the metamorphoses that were taking place with his city would feel even more severe. Several times in his visions, he would end up on the outskirts of the city where he grew up. He would look around and recognize nothing, even though, apparently, everything had remained the same as it was. And this, he would say to himself, is where you spent the first years of your life. These little streets swaddled in old wooden fences saw you grow into a person. You lived next to these people for decades. But is it really *them*, and not *others*? Because *others* are just the same people except with *other hearts* beating inside their bodies. How do you distinguish *them* from the *others*? How does the actual past differ from that which came to be here today?

***

Thinking about that, Habinsky languidly smiled at the face of his long-prized Odonata and slowly moved his legs, that is—fluttered them so as not to stagnate, that is, not to fester. The facet-like eyes of his lover looked simultaneously at him and at the rest of the world. Her whiskers stiffened. Her wings shimmered. She was experiencing pleasure. They say that men are not capable of simulating pleasure. So, keep this in mind: it's not true.

Turning his head a bit to the left, Haba saw how old men and women were sitting on the benches in the four-cornered, green courtyard, discussing the Right Sector's attack on their unhappy life, how children were laughing in the playground, how young drunks, student-aged, were sucking down beers while talking about Sartre and *russkii mir*,[10] how the magpies bickered, how the larks frolicked, and how smoke blew from the metallurgy plant. The blue sky hurled sheaves of gold sparks, cloaked itself in shallow cracks, and spilled downward, covering the ground with bronze ash.

She was, in essence, already leaving him, although she did not yet know it. Perhaps she was afraid of realizing that, as of now, she was attracted to a completely different world, one that, over the past few months, came to appear on the other side of the apartment's window. It contained various forms of life. In particular, those related to her—dragonflies.

He pondered whether anything would change if she were to leave her husband or, perhaps, give birth to a child. An answer arrived a few days later. In a certain reference book, Haba read a short explanatory article. A certain life sciences expert clearly described exactly that which Sosipatra was lately forcing him to do. It turns out that dragonflies generally mate while in flight—it's a completely natural phenomenon. But what's most

important is that the copulatory device of male dragonflies is marked by an extraordinary high specialization. It
is so high that it has no analogies in the world of insects.
Even the king of nature—sapiens sapiens—wasn't able
to come up with it. During mating, it is typical for the
male dragonfly to remove the sperm of his predecessor
(*the issue of "predecessors" in the Ukrainian political system
(sic!) is a purely biological phenomenon*), before carefully
and vigilantly leaving his own. Oh, fuck, Haba became
sullen. I never had a chance. When your lover craves sex
with insects, there is nothing you can do. Just recognize
it and let her go.

In April, they returned from the supermarket with
things for her birthday. She really wanted to have a party.
She dreamed about inviting a bunch of people, putting
on her favorite black dress, about being pretty, funny,
and attractive. She truly loved her birthdays, just like
she loved all the holidays sanctified by the local tradition.
Haba blew a lot of money on party drinks and food.

They were returning from the Metro supermarket.
Odonata fell asleep. Haba looked at her and was hit with
another attack of heavy doubt. While on Kyiv Avenue,
about ten minutes from home, Sosi suddenly began
shuddering and moaning, and then piercingly screamed.
Haba became a bit frightened and almost fainted right at
the steering wheel, but a part of him vigilantly and coolly
followed along with everything that was taking place. The
scene, to be honest, was not pleasant. In ordinary life,
an imago never transforms into a larva, that's pure nonsense. Every life science expert worth his salt will tell you
that, in order to have a larva, you need eggs. No matter

what you do, eggs are an essential phase in life (*you and I know about this, brother Hermes*).

But that's life. If anyone needed someone's eggs at that time, it was not Sosipatra. All she needed was the inside of an old car and the cigarettes that Haba would light up one after another for his lover until this thing let her go. On the back seat of Haba's old car, skipping the egg stage, his girl turned directly into a naiad.

The dead exuviae of the dear Sosi cooled on the back seat, holding a burning cigarette in its bare hands. It enlarged its eyes (*her eyes*) that were absolutely empty, offset, and glazed-over. And next to it lay a live, robust naiad. Generally speaking, one could, without question, see Sosipatra's face in its face. But it was a completely different creature nonetheless.

The city of changes changed his lover. She should have been taken away from here earlier, Haba thought much too late, at least half a year ago, maybe then she would have remained a person. During a sharp turn, the empty exuviae slid and slammed into the door, cracked in several places, and slowly spilled onto the floor.

Habinsky drove the naiad to the bank of the Kalmius River. He took it out of the car and put it by the water. A yellow-red wind was blowing, simultaneously cold and warm. On the opposite bank, the pro-Russian rallies would not abate and fragments of blistering slogans and fiery speeches would fly over here.

There were large black speakers booming near the regional administration building. "This is how it is now, dear brothers, difficult times have come ... tanks are approaching the Donbas, the faggots and the Banderites are in attack mode, they have chased the *proffesor-proffesor*

out of the country ... let us unite with other sapiens sapiens who think like we do ... let us strike back at that
kike-Banderite mob..."

These sentiments would reach them in segments, or,
more precisely, in chunks. The loudspeaker droned. Poems were read out loud—it was not clear which poems,
but it was definitely rhymed verse. At the very edge of his
consciousness, Habinsky realized that patriotism does
not like free verse. Then "Katiusha"[11] was sung. After that,
someone yelled something into the microphone.

Sosipatra dried up a bit and came to her senses. She
emerged from the scars of Chelidonium majus and
milkweed, and asked for a cigarette. Her voice, although
obviously different, was still recognizable. She smiled
listlessly and greedily grabbed a Marlborough. The wind
intensified and brought the lyrics of the song, carrying
them from the regional administration building across
the Kalmius River: "*and the accordion in the trenches sings to
me about your smile and your eyes.*"[12]

Sosipatra sucked the cigarette down to the filter, pensively looked at Haba, clenched her jaw, stuck out her
lower lip, captured a little frog that was carelessly climb-
ing onto the shore, and swallowed it. She glanced at Haba
somewhat frivolously, shook her head and suddenly sang
out: "Oh, my dear Kozak, what are we to do? Oh, oh-oh,
oh, oh, oh! Oh, we need a cradle, oh, my dear! From Kyiv
to Rostov, here and there, and there and here, a cradle
of bark, hark, hark-hark!"[13] and crawled into the water.

"I want you to hear," Haba responded, "how my living
voice grieves."[14]

"It's nothing, it'll pass," Sosipatra replied.

The water was grey all around the shores and would blacken towards the center. The wind picked up once again, chased the clouds, slammed the earth with large green waves. A lark flew by yelling happily and metallically. Haba pulled on his hood. The trees creaked; old dry branches spilled downward. And Sosipatra kept crawling and crawling, leaving a dark and slimy trail behind her.

"Will I see you at least one more time?" he yelled when the naiad touched the water with her body.

"No doubt, we will see each other one more time."

"That's all I need."

"And who knows if you will be happy that you did."

"When will it be?"

"When the Mare's Head gets to descriptive and relative pronouns," the naiad answered, made a bang, like a kid's drum, and tumbled into the water. Within a second there was no trace of Sosipatra on the surface of the water, not even one little circle.

"May God watch over you, my love," Haba shrugged his shoulders. (*Recall my sins, naiad, in your prayers. In your prayers, nymph, remember everything for which I am guilty.*)[15] He picked up the lighter that Sosipatra left on the shore, tossed it in his palm a few times, and then threw it into the Kalmius. Looking into the black-blue sky above the dancing tress, he headed for his car. This has nothing to do with either revolution or evolution, he thought to himself. These are just certain types of metamorphoses, complete transformations. It's best to just get used to it and not ask any unnecessary questions. Lightening blinded the eyes, as did a new paroxysm: "*Let noble anger rise like a wave...*"[16]

Haba sat down behind the wheel, placed his head in his hands and quietly cried. Streams of water slammed onto the roof of the car with a roar. The downpour had finally begun.

Conditionalis

Deep in reflection, Sancho figured that he had travelled half a mile or more when he noticed something ahead that looked like daylight coming though some kind of opening—this path, which he regarded as the road to the other world, was to finally lead him out of here.

—Servantes, *The Ingenious Hidalgo Don Quixote of La Mancha*

In nature, there exists a Minsk market, but there is also a market near the Heroïv Dnipra metro station, and one needs to distinguish between the two. The latter one is about a mile and a half from home, but it is nonetheless better to go to that one. One can always get a good deal on cured fat and other homemade delicacies there, which are brought in from the villages and small towns of the Kyiv region. For example: nice, still warm milk; colostrum; and buckwheat honey. Haba never had enough money to buy everything that he wanted, but he did have a system.

If he were to buy a chunk of cured fat this Saturday, then next Saturday, for example, he'll get a ring of sausage and a head of garlic. And, on Friday, he'll pick up some milk that is still warm.

"My cow isn't just any cow, it's a sorceress," the old yellow man says (*that's how the teacher Zhuangzi probably looked*), nodding a request for a cigarette, lighting up, and blowing out some smoke with great satisfaction. "This cow's grandma was named Mathilde von d'Este. People would say that she was a direct descendent of the Hapsburgs. (*Once, I, Zhuang Zhou, dreamt that I was a butterfly—a happy butterfly freely fluttering among the flowers, and I didn't know that...*)[1] This cow did so many good things for our family. We, just so you know, live in Publiieve-Neronove. It's over thirty-seven miles away from Kyiv. But that's not important. Mathilde turned out to be so wise that, for twenty years in a row, she worked as secretary for the local branch of the Communist Party, ran the library, and served as the head of the local forest ministry for several years. And no surprise there—blue blood always reveals itself in the end."

"The cow worked as a secretary for the local branch of the Communist Party?" Haba repeated to himself quite seriously. "In Publiieve-Neuronove?"

"First of all—there is no need to say 'Neuronove,' because it makes you think of neurons, which have nothing to do with this. There are no neurons, brother, in this world. It's fiction, a fake term. Don't ever mention neurons to anybody. No one in the Kyiv region will understand you."

"So how do you pronounce it?"

"Publiieve-Neronove. You, perhaps, have heard of the poet, Ovid (*Publius Ovidius Naso*).

"Yep, I've heard of him." Haba nodded. "And as for Neron, is it that one?"

"Yes, Nero (*Nero Claudius Caesar Augustus Germanicus*), at birth—Lucius Domitius Ahenobarbus, between 50 and 54 AD—Nero Claudius Caesar Drusus Germanicus. And in our parts (*the Kyiv region*) he was simply known as Nero. Nero is Nero, the Roman emperor, the last in the Julio-Claudian dynasty."

"I don't see any such town on the map," Habinsky said broodingly, looking at his phone.

"That's what I have been telling you, on the map it exists by its new name—Klavdiieve-Tarasove.[2] But everyone knows the old, authentic name—Publiieve-Neronove."

"So why did they suddenly change the name?"

"Well, it's because we are undergoing de-communization these days. Someone decided that it sounded too imperialistic. They did, however, maintain the mention of Nero. And it's Klavdiieve because it's the Julio-Claudian dynasty. And they got rid of the Publius part, no matter how hard our old heads argued against it. They were told that one of their own poets is just as good."

"Do you have in mind..."[3]

"Yes, or course, who else would we have in mind. And that is how it turned out a bit weird. But all of the locals continue to refer to it as Publiieve-Neronove."

"I'll have to come check it out someday."

"How much do you want, son? Two, three liters?" the old man asks with hope.

"Give me three."

The sun shines clearly and confidently. Habinsky pays the man.

"Ok, fine. But how could a cow have worked as a secretary for the party organization, even if it was in Neronove, even if it was in Soviet times? (*Lord Yuan of Sung once dreamed about a person with long, tousled hair, who came out of the side door of the hall and said...*)"[4]

"So then," the old man counts the money twice and puts them in his greasy, cloth wallet, "everyone was amazed. People even came from Moscow to see our Mathilde when she was chosen to be a deputy in the Twentieth All-Union Congress of the Communist Party of the Soviet Union. Alright then, come by again. I need to start getting out of here."

"Ok," Haba nods, "I gotta go, too. (*I am a marine messenger attached to the staff of the River God Hebo. A fisherman, named Yü, has caught me.*)[5] You see, I am a refugee. And that is why I believe everything that is told to me. Because I have some experience, too. I can tell you some things as well."

"What do you have in mind?" the old man looks at him suspiciously.

"Well, I thought of this while I was listening to you. In my early childhood, you see, early in the morning, the birds had not yet awoken and a cow (*which had belonged to my late grandmother Marfa Oleksandrivna*) named Haida would enter the orchard in a white shirt and sing Donizetti arias in a high-pitched voice. She was so good at it that dead coalminers crawled out from underground and listened to her for hours. They listened and cried. And that is what is known as art."

An unpleasant, difficult pause got stranded in the air.

"You must be from Donetsk, right?"

"From no other place, but there (*having woken up, the Lord Yuan wanted to know what his dream was about. The dream interpreter said: "this is a numinous turtle"*).[6]

"Well, I can see that." The old man picked up his bag and, without saying bye, quickly headed for the bus stop.

And that's how it always goes. Solitude is the worst thing about this wonderful city. A person born in the Donbas carries it within them, somewhere in the *plexus coeliacus* or, more likely, even in the stomach, like Coca-Cola mixed with vodka, two parts to one. That person is, in essence, that very same numinous turtle, which does not know whether it is a Chinese philosopher or a Ukrainian butterfly.

The sun shone, and the wind blew into the languid brain. Haba carried the milk home. He thought of yesterday's (*yet to take place*) meeting with Ole.

***

They leisurely drank the cognac, laughed, and conversed nonchalantly and freely. The big difference in our ages, he thought, and in our political and philosophical preferences does not bother us at all. Her little eyes shine, the Ukrainian language just pours out of her petite, round mouth, her little teeth loom white, her every move, every smile seems so refined, so measured (*you think, young Kozak, that I am dying in vain, but I am, young man, controlling your brain*).[7] It's been so long, Haba deliberated exaltedly, so long since I've had a conversation that was so beautiful and beneficial.

Habinsky was happy for quite a while. Maybe for two hours, or maybe for whole three. It was now clear that this was not a chance meeting. And this long evening, with its Baltic clouds, rain, which had no interest in stopping, and with its cold and penetrating evening wind, was also not just fortuitous. No, this girl is not just some random creature on my life path, Haba thought enthusiastically. And everything that we ate and drank was not consumed by us accidentally, but in the proportions that were necessary in order to move slowly, but at the same time—headlong, or, as they say—a bit bent over, in a steady, warm, and promising direction. For the first time in a while, Habinsky felt like he truly desired something, in a concrete sense. And what person in his shoes wouldn't? And just in that moment, when Habinsky had definitively figured everything out for himself, the stool next to him became occupied by the Mare's Head.

"By the way," it said, taking off its wet hat, "it's already cold outside. I am tired of waiting for you, boy, but, whatever—as you wish."

Habinsky was pretending that he hadn't heard anything.

"I see that you are not the politest of dudes," the MR noticed, "but what can you do," it swiftly grabbed a sausage sandwich from his plate and began to chew (*gnaw, munch*) and periodically, in a very ladylike fashion, coquettishly nibble. "You and I have a Ukrainian language lesson scheduled. And in your life language is paramount. Whether you want to or not, I'm going to make sure you learn it. In a few years, you will have developed such an impressive lexicon that the late Lukash would be jealous.[8] You'll see."

Haba twitched his wide cheek bones, pressed his lips, and tightly closed his eyes. If he had been just a little bit less fond of Ole, he would have gotten up, bid farewell, and left. But there was hope that the MR would back off if he would just ignore it.

"Ok then, let's begin," the insatiable maned scoundrel dreamily droned and grabbed a poppy cookie. "So, we have established that a verb is an independent element of language that describes an action or state, and that answers questions. What questions? Well, all of them, I guess..."

"I'm begging you. Get out of here," Habinsky requested, attempting to speak as calmly as possible. "We'll get together at home and discuss everything. Verbs, adjectives, pronouns, Sosiura and Semenko, Drach and Franko.[9] Get away from me, please, oh my blessed joy."

"Excuse me?" Luk-Oie raised her eyebrows.

"Forgive me," Habinsky jerked his shoulders, "I was not referring to you."

"To whom, then?"

"Compared to Proto-Slavic and Old Ukrainian," the MR continued, "the contemporary Ukrainian language has a simple verbal system... Listen, grab me a cherry *pliatsok*—this cognac really makes me crave something sweet..."

"Forgive me, I should have forewarned you, but I was hoping that we could avoid this douche bag." Haba pulled out a handkerchief and wiped his sweaty face. "The fact is, it is next to us. It is, as they say, among us."

"What is, Habriel Bohdanovych?" Ole became anxious and carefully looked around.

"Just hear me out and then you can leave for good, ok?" Habinsky asked. "Just hear me out. That's all that I ask for (*and an accordion in the trenches sings to me*)."[10]

"That's fine, no problem, no need to panic," Ole glanced around again, "is it an old acquaintance of yours?"

"You could say so," Habinsky nodded.

"Why don't we just get out of here? I think it's too early to go home. But there are a bunch of nearby places where we could sit down and continue our conversation. What do you think?"

The Mare's Head hadn't stopped speaking for a second during all this and continued the lesson in a soft and pleasant baritone. It would only stop occasionally now to take a sip of cognac out of Haba's glass:

"...and the ending *-ši was formed out of the older *-si (through –*-xi). And this, my boy, is all the first palatalization. And so, to put it briefly, the pluperfect and perfect remained. Let us continue. Participles decline the same way that adjectives of the hard group do..."

"The thing is," Haba tried to focus with all his might, "that it's impossible to get away from this beast."

"Is it some kind of woman?"

"In a certain sense, yes," he agreed, giving the MR's thick mane the stink-eye.

"Well, then, I guess, I pretty much get it," the girl sighed, almost out of relief.

"...conditionalis, the Latin—modus conditionalis, from condition, which means 'condition,'—a grammatical tense which speculates what we wish would happen or could happen under certain conditions."

"I would prefer to never see you again in any condition!" Habinsky slammed the table. "I implore you, go away, give me a break!"

The glass flipped over onto the saucer. The tea spilled over along the table and began pouring onto the floor.

Their table caught the attention of everyone present. Habinsky sensed that he had finally lost his composure.

"Fine," the Mare's Head agreed after taking a dramatic pause, "go. We'll look at this as an opportunity for you to practice your language. But I'll go with the two of you. Because someone has to watch over you."

"Yes, we do need to go," Haba stood up, "if that's ok with you, of course. We can talk somewhere else."

"We can speak some other time, if you're *that busy*," Ole said with unpleasant astonishment and glanced at her watch.

"Please," he almost methodically took her little, warm palm, looking into her eyes with wonder, "let's continue talking. About Galicia, about Chernivtsi, about folk dolls, or about other lofty, heavenly, and uplifting things. You spoke about them so enchantingly. It even made me want to live there, perhaps for a bit, perhaps with someone. You know, occasionally I would get a desire to come to Western Ukraine on a whim and live there amongst the locals for some time. Like a dead man among the living," he became silent for a minute, "but then, occasionally, the other way around. Sometimes it's the other way around."

Haba settled the check, and they got dressed and went out to Iaroslaviv Val. Haba and Ole popped open their umbrellas and unhurriedly headed for the metro.

"Your acquaintance stayed behind in Iaroslavna, right? Then why are you so sad?"

"The thing is," Habinsky said, "a star shone upon me this morning, thrusted through my window. And grace lay on my gloomy soul so brightly that I blissfully understood: that star is just a splinter of pain stretched out eternally, as if by fire."[11]

"And that is what I love about you," the MR gently mumbled behind him, "you have a vast and ridiculous memory."

"Excuse me, Ole, I have such a complicated and, you know, unstable life. I am very sorry about what happened in Iaroslavna."

"Don't be sad," Ole looked at him in an unexpectedly tender way, "that's life."

"You know, for hundreds (*thousands?*) of days in a row now my fate rolls along, sometimes up and sometimes down. So many months have passed since I left my city and moved here, and I still cannot find my bearings. And you know what," Haba noticed an inevitable elevation in his emotions and almost began crying, "I get it: most of what I see every day, almost every minute, takes place only in my mind. Most of the emotions and words that I express, most of my efforts are redundant, superfluous, useless, silly, and trite. No one from the intellectual circles wants to converse with me because I never say that which needs to be said, or maybe I don't say it the right way, or perhaps I am not in the proper emotional state. And I never bring up the right topics. But, instead, those who no one really cares about. So, I'm sitting next to someone. And I really want to tell them something good, beautiful, and beneficial; to express, to pour my love into simple and clear statements that will help them to understand how important it is for me that they, an extraordinary individual, are with me at this time. And that's the way it should be—telling people that you're happy to be present in existence, together with them..."

"It is very good that you feel that way!"

"You think so?" Haba sighed. "But instead of saying all of that, I say something different. I start going off about the phenomenal similarity of mental creations such as "I," "number," and "straight line," or for naught I bring up all kinds of philosophers (*who, by the way, should have been left alone a long time ago, they didn't start this war*). I say all these things and think: "Habriel, man, chill out, what are you doing!"

"And so, Habriel?"

"And nothing," Habinsky shrugged his shoulders, "it's always the same. I come out looking stupid, or incompetent, or sometimes, perhaps, phony. Excessive and insane—every time. Moreover... the problem is that I cannot control this process in any manner. Correction: When I remain completely silent, then I can. But as soon as I begin speaking, you can kiss any normal discussion good-bye. Perhaps I truly do need to see a psychiatrist..."

"But didn't you say that you already do?"

"I lied," Habinsky immediately admitted his fault.

"What for?" Ola smiled.

"And I lied about this to Petro Petrovych several times, too," Haba confessed. "Because I know that he is genuinely concerned. And I don't blame him. Anyone would start to worry, especially if your assistant sees, in the middle of a fancy supermarket, foxes and monkeys, who are buying alcohol, cleaning products, oranges, hairy fruits from the southern hemisphere, and pigs and hedgehogs, who like candy, rice, and potatoes..." He fell silent, thinking about something for a second. "Even horses. Aleko, for example."

"Who's Aleko?"

"Oh, never mind," Habinsky couldn't come up with a reply. "You know what? As soon I even begin to think about a trip to a medical facility, I experience a shortness of breath."

***

You really should go see a psychiatrist, Lionia—who lived on the second floor together with his old mother and a kitty named Kitty—recommended. Habinsky would sometimes seek out Lionia. The latter was capable of taking care of a sink, electricity, could install a toilet or a boiler, replace a tank, fix a closet door, and a whole bunch of other stuff. Such individuals are sent by Providence to refugees of all ages so that they can survive in some manner. Lionia was a good dude but would only accept payment by pricey alcohol. And he preferred to consume the little bottle together with someone. And, of course, Haba also shared with him everything that he thought about in those Kyiv days that were long, like dreams.

"Do not talk to anyone besides me," Lionia would continually say after their get-togethers, "about your past (*future?*), may God save you! Me, I am a simple man, I understand these things. You are a luminary, and an educated *individuality*. Moreover, one from the Donbas. A zone of double risk. I take this all into account and that is why I interact with you calmly and responsibly. Others wouldn't treat you in this manner. Except for, maybe, a psychiatrist. Why not give it a shot, Haba? We have such a good clinic here. Pavlo Pavlovych works there. He is able to help people in ways that no one has ever helped us before. When I'm feeling bad, I always sign up for an appointment with him. After two-three chats, I am able to stop drinking for a month. I tell you, he's not just Dr. Paul, he's St. Paul."

It is quiet in the office. An overfilled ashtray sits on the windowsill. The doctor—a bald, mustached, hefty dude—writes something in his journal. It smells either like chlorine or like carbolic acid, or perhaps like both simultaneously. And with a bit of an electric current and some ozone mixed in. It's as if bolts of lightning had struck this room a minute before Haba entered it. In other offices down the corridor, patients shout and cry. On the other side of the wall, someone tearfully preys to St. Sebastian.

"What's going on over there?" Haba gestures towards the wall.

"Ah," the doctor smiles, "it's the state dentists working on the refugees. Pay no attention to it. Let us remain silent and focused."

"Focused on what?" a somewhat nervous Habinsky impatiently inquires. He hadn't had much experience with psychiatrists, so he does not know how to properly behave. Pavlo Pavlovych ignores the question and quietly places his hand on the table. He is silent. He looks at Haba sternly, piercingly, unremittingly. And later, just when Haba, no longer able to handle the nervous pressure, begins to fall asleep, he quietly asks:

"So, what is it that you want from me, son?"

"Lionia," Habinsky responds, sharply sensing his insignificance as well as the dry saliva that suddenly begins to scratch his throat, "advised me to see you. Lionia, the local handyman. He said that you, like no one else, know the cerebral, as well as, perhaps, the cerebrospinal,

matters of a human. That you know how much dopa-
mine, how many substances, endorphins, phobias, and
procrastinations are needed by a human. That you know
what differentiates a normal quattrocento Ukrainian[12]
from a ressentiment one..."[13]

"Slow down," Pavlo raises his hefty hand. "Don't rush.
It's your first visit. I see that the etiology of your sickness
is complex. It needs to be understood. And we will do that
quietly but also determinately. Do you agree that deter-
mination and quiet are our most important friends?"

"Yes, in this office, at least," Haba answers, carefully choosing his words and ashamedly looking out
the window.

The Lord's Cross suddenly forms in the Obolon sky.
A cluster of Ukrainian Angels appears around it with sad,
yet gentle, national faces and with small, yet bright, yellow and blue wings.[14] They nod their heads in a very kind
fashion. As if saying: listen to the doctor, he is a saintly
man, whatever he says, you do. "I am just a simple Christian man," Haba wanted to reply to the Angels, "who is
very upset about the latest events taking place in the
Ukrainian universe, which is under your control. Besides
that, I'm not that young anymore, so there's not much
left for me to do. I really don't have much of a choice, but,
my beloved Angels, the screams that I hear behind the
walls of this clinic do make my hair stand on end. The holy
Obolon inquisition is an absolute horror." But he did not
end up saying this. Instead, he decided to kiss up to those
in power, just in case, and whispered "Glory to Ukraine!"
"Glory to Its Heroes!" the Lord's Angels replied in a quiet,
yet powerful, choir and formed a giant *tryzub* in the sky.[15]

Haba turned away from the widow out of fright, and his eyes once again met Pavlo Pavlovych's.

The latter was fastidiously studying Haba's physiognomy. After a moment of involved deliberations, the doctor surmised: "Let us start at the top. Pronouns can be substantive. First of all, we have all the personal pronouns: 'I,' 'we,' 'you,' 'you' (pl.), 'he,' 'she,' 'it,' and 'they.' Secondly, the reflexive pronoun, 'myself,' and the interrogative pronouns: 'who' and 'what.' Next, we need to designate the indefinite pronouns, for example, 'someone,' 'something,' 'somewhat,' 'anybody,' and 'anything'; and what's left are only the negative pronouns like 'no one,' 'none,' 'nobody,' and 'nothing.' That's basically it," Pavlo Pavlovych smiles and takes a drag. "Shall I mention the attributive and numerical ones, or do you know them?"

"I am familiar with them," Haba shrugged his shoulders, "can I light up as well?"

"Well, why not, feel at home," the doctor pushed the pack of smokes to the edge of the table.

Habinsky thrust the cigarette into his mouth with trembling fingers and ignited the lighter about five times. Finally, he inhaled.

"It was cool, the way you dealt with them," he decided to kiss up to the doctor, aiming the blue stream of smoke perpendicular to the ceiling.

"With the pronouns?"

"Yep, with them. I was especially enamored with 'someone,' 'something,' 'somewhat,' 'anybody,' and 'anything.' I couldn't have pulled that off."

"Yes, that is the result of many difficult years of work with various patients. The ressentiment matter is a little more difficult, I'll get to that later, it would be better to begin with the *Quattrocento*. In general, it is something that continues to this day. The High Renaissance has already extinguished itself, and the Enlightenment turned into the post-industrial revolution. They've already buried God and then found him again in these parts of the world, and perspective—the most important discovery of the quattrocento—remains the only adequate instrument for a thinking person of the simple refugee type.[16] Do you know what perspective is?"

"Well, I think I know, I guess so," Haba replied carefully.

"Yeah, right, who is it that I am asking about perspective," the doctor sadly shook his head. "What kind of perspective could you have, you poor chap. None, brother, none. (*They woke the centurion and told him: it's like this, like that! The poor chap makes the sign of the cross, gets on the best horse, and gallops away to Kyiv.*)[17] And you are poor, too. Neither here, nor there. I get it, no prospects, such is life. But keep in mind that the character of depicting things, shaped by the length of their distance from the viewer is, in essence, perspective. In our clinic, Ambrogio Lorenzetti[18] is considered to be the one who discovered it, which is why we, including you, are so thankful to him. And, be it as it may, I don't have any other perspective for you."

"Understood," Haba shrugged.

"And regarding ressentiment, one needs to be careful. Because that thing is deceptive, like the prices in Karma-Town. Do you shop at our shopping and entertainment center, son?"

"Occasionally, yes," Habinsky said, "but I prefer going to Heroïv Dnipra. It's much simpler there: salted pork, eggs, Zhuang Zhou butterflies, Mathilde von d'Este, and solid decent people. And there are no neurons in the Kyiv region, at least you shouldn't think about them if you want to be understood by others. And I try not to talk about, or to even think about such things..."

"Try not to, try not to," Pavlo Pavlovych approvingly nodded his head. "Because that resentment, those grudges that accompany a person who, holding his final pennies in his hand, moves between that hellish skating rink and that dolphin Tolia—we don't need them. Let's take, for example, brother Hermes Trismegistus: what is he if not a reliable sign of your ressentiment?"

"Leave Hermes alone," Haba got offended, "there's nothing wrong with him."

"Well, there you have it. And you're going to tell me that there is nothing wrong with me, too?"

"Yes, of course, unless it is proven otherwise, I believe that you are a good person."

"But I am not a person at all, my boy," Pavlo Pavlovych sighs, and begins to dim and melt in front of his eyes. "Although, unfortunately, it's a shame, it really is a shame..."

***

"You don't need to go anywhere," Ole quietly said, "you just lack normal conversations on a consistent level...You've turned around now for the second time. What is it?"

"You're right, but it's still here," Haba disclosed, "it is following behind me and may never leave me alone."

"There is nothing there," Ole said calmly. "Are you making this up on purpose," Ole piercingly looked into his eyes, "to prevent this evening from actually resulting in something concrete? Are you afraid of my uncle? Well, don't be, he'll be fine with it if something should take place. Or, maybe, it is me that you are afraid of? Or are you already sorry that you invited me over here? Just let me know, I'll be fine with it."

For a moment Haba came down with Syndrome 33 (*too many questions*), but he was able to regain his balance, although he did give off a nervous yawn (*I invited her? Really?*).

"What a vapid chick," the diagnosis was provided by the MR, who was keeping up behind them.

"The Mare's Head," Habinsky decided to remain frank throughout, "have you heard of it?"

"I have," Ole smiled.

"Well, that is what is walking with us now, just a few steps behind us."

"Metaphorically?" Ole laughed genuinely. "I'll probably never get used to your sense of humor! You sure are a unique person."

"It's not about metaphors," Haba fatedly looked at the sky. The clouds were not scattering. The wind crashed into the buildings, hurtled clumps of leaves and tiny, multi-colored stars into bright and dark windows. A nice dark wind, a Guinness Draught wind.

"Fine, you two go ahead then," the Mare's Head finally decided, "but keep in mind, Hamlet, that there was no naiad and, moreover, there was no nymph."

***

Sosipatra had found for herself, figuratively speaking, a Guildenstern, a shamisen instructor, a top specialist in surveying, and, by the way, a professional linguist. This happened because of her youthfulness and because of your permanent foolhardiness. She would still visit you for some time, according to her previous memory, but a new memory was forming in her, as were exciting new attractions.

However, a month after she finally did leave you, someone suffocated her with a scarf—with her own scarf—halfway between the bus stop and your building. They never found the killer and, actually, no one looked for him. By then thugs were regularly patrolling the streets of the city. Who cared about the death of some funny little girl? You had gotten sick of going over to meet with investigator Piven...

"Piven?" Habinsky crinkled his forehead.

Yes, Major Piven and First Lieutenant Khrobachenko.[19] Ethnic Ukrainians, by the way. Great guys. It is with these two city representatives of the Ukrainian Ministry of Internal Affairs that you tried to negotiate with. In a scholarly, investigative, law-breaking as well people's-life-protecting sense. You needed to know who killed your little lady and why it was done with such a light—like a nighttime breeze—scarf, the one you bought for her at the start of spring? And if there was a need to murder someone, then why was it done just a few steps from your building? Why, after she was killed, the killer didn't place her on one of those beautiful benches that are found all along Mr. Pushkin's Boulevard, but instead tossed her, just like that, between those flowerbeds filled with dahlias, carnations, grenadines, and large bushes of lilac? Was the pose in which they left her after her death accidental? What were her final words, thoughts, and wishes?

In other words, you had a whole list of questions and all of them fucked with your little, provincial brain. You cried when you were alone and looked at all of her funny multi-colored things scattered about the apartment. You sniffed her panties, you dove into them, like a very old, half-dead whale dives into familiar depths of the Pacific Ocean for the last time, sensing that he is gone for good. From your heart to your damp eyes rose the scent of her sweat and deodorant. The buzz of her wings, the tinkle of her urine. Compared to them, Bach's Prelude and Fugue in F Minor is junk. Large ears and feet, small breasts, and tiny, funny hands. Yellow panties, blue socks, blue panties, and a yellow sock.

One of them asked you for a thousand dollars, saying that he knew who did it. He said he would take care of everything and would answer all your questions. You gave him the money. Two weeks later you asked to meet again with the representatives of law and order, but you were not allowed into their office. You waited in the corridor. Then you waited by the entrance to the precinct. You finally caught up with them in the evening, but you would have been better off not doing that. They really did a number on you, but you managed to stay alive.

Then you tried to get some answers on your own. Sosipatra's friends supposedly saw, in the afternoon by the university building, an orange cap pursuing the light, small, funny figure of your former lover in the crowd. Caps like that are not rare, guys such as that are not rare, especially in today's times. Every third guy today is a real clown.

But then May arrived. She had almost made it to the anniversary of your relationship. At the end of the month, you purchased a train ticket to Kyiv and got out of there.

In the days before your departure, you took a bus to her village. Without delay, you set off for the home of the deceased. Yes, you easily figured out which way to go, although you had never been there before (*traces of her are destined to eternally flicker along these little paths, the scent of Chinese perfumes can only be eliminated by chemical weapons, non-obligating shadows of others' memories, and quiet female laughter*), and went there. Suddenly, right by the entrance to the village store, you ran into her former husband.

You recognized him right away. He was dressed in a *sarafan*, with a *kokoshnik* on top of his orange cap, wearing authentic Russian shoes, and carrying a huge red bag full of samovars and Orthodox icons with his strong male hands.[20] An AK-47 could be seen bobbling behind his back.

"*We worship flesh—its taste and its color*," he sang in Russian. "*Oh, stench of death—we are in awe. We're not to blame for crushing your bones in our tough and tender Russian paws.*"[21] He hummed these beautiful words, which came from the depths of his heart, to the melody of that famous city (*across Russified cities*) ballad (*and you didn't come again today*).[22] You smiled at him genuinely and then killed him with two strikes right into the heart (*beginner's luck*). And, who knows why, you took home the bloody knife (*you had used it to peel fruits for Sosipatra*) and one of the Tula samovars (*fully functional, made in Tula, copper, wood-burning, 1896, with 21 medals on the cover, 8 by the spout*) that were covered with blood, and did not even try to wash them or throw them out until morning. You took a shower and, until almost 3 am, wrapped in a bedsheet, you sat in the kitchen, examined the doubtless proof of your act, drank cold dry wine, and grieved.

The MR was thinking: "It is not for me to judge you, brother, as God is my witness, not for me. But, boy, I now think it is quite possible that Sosi's life was taken away not by her husband but, let's say, by her father. Just between us, he's got a few screws loose, too."

"Her father?" Haba asked barely audibly.

"But, in the end, what do we care? What's important is that you got vengeance. With this family, with this *russkii mir.* Isn't that worth it?"

"Worth it?" Haba repeated with dry lips.

"Well, I don't know," the MR licked its lips. "You know better. Either way, you have become a killer, my friend, you violated God's commandment. And I congratulate you on that. And awaiting you now are the flames of hell or, as another possibility, getting lost in the ceaseless tunneled universe—both today's and tomorrow's—of the Kyiv metro system."

"A Mare's Head?" Ola asked amidst this and laughed out loud. "You truly are an extraordinary person. You have the imagination of three PhDs!"

"With enough remaining for seven more," the MR added and quietly dissolved in the air.

"So, Miss Ole," Haba stepped on the throat of his own doubt and closed his umbrella, "shall we go to my place?"

***

But we are, of course, getting a bit ahead of ourselves. Or, perhaps, we're running behind. A person runs behind very often. Runs behind and then laughs like a monkey. Because it thinks it has gotten ahead of everyone. And that darling doesn't understand that its spiritual frontier (*a population density of less than two people per quarter mile*) is located in its own ass. But that's not what we are talking about here. It goes without saying that Ukrainian language lessons for the refugee-polyglot could not have begun before that long-awaited meeting had taken place in this novel. And now we need to somehow imagine it. Moreover, we can only imagine those things that have already taken place. Unfortunately, imagination, in general, does not work with that which has not taken place, or that is not present.

So, then. Having already gotten a bit used to the new surroundings, and having placed candles in front of the Mother Mary and St. Nicholas on the days before the Sabbath, Haba realized that a modest party was now in order. A homey and quiet one, with clouds outside the window, with a cigarette and a certain number of drinks, with a light dinner, with a quiet sorrow, and with the eleven-volume *Dictionary of the Ukrainian Language* (or DUL-11),[23] which was published in the 1970s and 80s. So then, the DUL, drinks, dinner, and jazz music on the radio. But there was no one to invite, nor was there any reason to invite them. Lionia was in the middle of week-long bender, didn't leave his apartment, and didn't open his door, so he was not an option.

Saturday turned out to be rainy. It thundered and roared in the morning and lightning bolts were landing somewhere in the distance, and the Dnipro river, of course, did not bellow,[24] it had no need for that. It just mumbled something (*when you play cards or drink wine*

*from a glass, my friend, and are married feverishly to a heavy
fog dizziness, make sure you don't pay too much for this minute,
when your shadow (Aleko?) abandons you and will become your
enemy)*[25] reflective and philosophical. At this moment, we
hear a ten-hole chromatic *sopilka*[26] and a trio of steady
contra basses.

The mention of the shadow here is very appropriate
because it was on this Saturday that Hermes did not want
to look at Haba in the mirror and turned his face away. At
7 am, when Habinsky was shaving, Hermes carefully provided an obedient reflection for only a few seconds, and
then sat at the edge of the tub and lit up a smoke, sadly
looking in the window (*with the eleventh*), which was not
reflected in the mirror. But Haba knew that, wherever it
was that Hermes was sitting, there was a window there
just like his. Why are you looking away, you force of evil?
Is my face no longer good enough for you?

Birds and fish are becoming aggravated by the drops
in atmospheric pressure, Hermes announced, flicking
ash off his cigarette into the tub. The young mothers from
the second, seventh, and ninth building entrance, who
had always taken their kids out for strolls together, starting at 8 am, will decide not to go outside today. I can see
that, said Haba, so what? The Mare's Head is close by, son,
Hermes said, stood up, rinsed his shaven face, and stuck
out his tongue at Haba. Don't try to scare me, Habinsky
retorted, wiped himself with a towel and went into the
room. He carefully closed the doors behind him. He became pensive for a moment and, bringing three fingers
together, made the sign of the cross in front of the doors
a few times. A quiet laughter leaked from the bathroom.
Why don't you cross your ass (*worries are married feverishly*

to a heavy fog),[27] Trismegistus almost advised, and it got quiet. There was only the wind outside the window. Only the smell of the Dnipro and of McDonald's from the balcony.

He was making dinner for two hours, singing along to "There Is a High Mountain."[28] When he would get to that part about the "three willows," his imagination, no matter how hard he tried to be proper, always drew only two. And the willows weren't really willows either, brother, but two genuine black poplars. A couple of *Populus nigra*, three hundred and thirty-five yards tall, a wide crown, a thick trunk, and a dense dark-grey, crack-filled bark. Its buds contain tar, natural gum, minerals, essential oil, and both malic and Gallic acids. And, considering the state that Haba had been in for the past few months, he should have been consuming these buds every day. Oh, anti-inflammatory black poplar! Antimicrobic, pain-reducing, and bloodletting poplar. What do you think about when you are standing on the shore in a quiet place, where boats are docked? What do you pine for? But for real, what could you long for, my darling, you are so beneficial and beautiful already, unlike a person singing about the warm summer that will never come again and, perhaps, never existed. How many wounds, cuts, rashes, and bruised areas have you healed, *Populus nigra*. How many human souls have you led onto that shore of the dark river, this warm, dark Lethe, with its rolling waves, turning into the Danube, the Dnipro, the Buh, the Zbruch, the Kalmius, the Prut, and the Dnister rivers?

He almost burned the fish, but didn't. The salad turned out to be tasty and beneficial, although not very beautiful. Pieter Bruegel's paintings, for example, are much more beautiful, and thus have a much stronger effect. But to sit at a table at 4 pm, an empty one, to which no one but Haba was invited, was a bit creepy. Habinsky walked up to the balcony, thrusted the doors wide open and, looking at the wind and the clouds, said: come to me all you who can hear and know, and who have forgotten themselves. Come along the wind, along the water, from the South and the North, on a lone bird, on a blue cloud, in a person or, at least, in their memories of you.

Returning to the hall, little Habriel (*as was completely foreseen*) saw the Mare's Head on the old, worn couch. The beast had just placed a huge piece of fish on its plate. Upon seeing Haba, it immediately finished chewing the chunk, wiped its lips with a napkin, abruptly got up and took its hat off its head. Habinsky felt a bit dizzy and leaned on a stool to keep his balance. Like in childhood times, the MR was about three yards taller than him. It had the strong smell of a horse, thickly intermixed with some other steady and pleasant smell (*an oil-spray for everyday use, does not contain alkali, safe on plastic, wood, painted and lacquered surfaces, and safe for bluing*).

"Howdy, Mare's Head," he said simply and took a step towards it.

"My dearest one," the MR said emotionally and embraced him (*he swung his legs in the air*). "My virtuous one," (*he buried his face in the thick and long mane*). "My stupid one."

At that moment, Haba considered whether he should suddenly start crying (*underneath the eleventh*).

"Cut it out," the Head said sternly, "don't even think about it! Recall your father's face, young gun."

"Should I also recall the Bradis Table?" Habinsky began feebly resisting the strong embrace. "Let me get down, you beast, and sit in a chair."

"I say, you sure do have some great butter here in Kyiv," the MR fell into the crumpled sofa, began picking bones out of the fish and sucking on each and every one of them with great pleasure.

"You gotta go to Heroïv Dnipra to get the good butter," Habinsky advised and poured a couple of drinks.

"For cleaning and oiling," the MR explained, "it makes it easier to clean weapons."

"I always did wonder why you smelled like that."

"What can you say, its wartime."

"I don't know how to kill."

"Tell me more," the MR remarked, "whether you like it or not. And I'll listen."

Habinsky felt sorrow. The mare's eyes, as dark as night, looked at him piercingly and ironically.

"What do you say we have a drink," Habinsky offered.

"Without a doubt, and then we'll pour another," the MR agreed, "because this fairytale will keep us up until morning."

"What do you mean?"

"What do you mean, what do I mean?" the MR downed the shot and lit up a cigarette, poisonous, green smoke hung above the table in circles. "About children."

"What children? What are you talking about?"

"What do you mean, what children? The older one, Lida, is six. The twins Mariana and Lesia are five. The two brothers—Oleksii and Ivan—remained together to the end of their lives."

***

Multi-colored stars were spilled onto the sky. They sparkled and looked on as children warmed themselves at the white and yellow flames. The smoke twisted and their short lived-through life wrapped around that which, in the morning, was still their family home (*Oh, in twisted valleys of Lubny, in a high castle*).[29] They sat by the glowing logs of the former porch (*the burned bodies of their parents lay on the other side*), when, out of the darkness of the snowy riverside mounds, Markus the Pilgrim rose up to the smoldering ruins (*the lavish Prince Iaruma sits on the yew porch*). An old man. His little eyes glistened, sitting deep in his skull, which was tightly swathed in his brown skin (*the silent monk has lived for one hundred and twenty years*), and the wind blew his no longer-really-white but already-almost-green beard.

He stood silently for a minute, looking around, and only then walked up to the children. Without saying anything, he embraced the oldest one, Lida. Mariana and Lesia, in turn, hugged him themselves.

"Poor things! They must be cold."

"We are cold," Ivan cried. "There," he pointed with his finger, "our parents lie there..."

"They are not there, there is nobody there anymore! Don't cry, young boy, on an empty stomach, it's not good," Markus picked Ivan up onto his arms. "Eat some porridge, drink some milk, I still have half a liter, it will warm you up, and after that we will embrace and cry together. Come to me, children. But stay quiet, first go along the coastline and then along the ice floe. There is no path to the footbridge. I don't want anyone from the village to see us."

And they set out (*and they call him the savior Movchal-nyk*).[30] Upon the snows, on narrow paths, under the flashes of the starlight that clustered and twinkled in dark-blue and yellow patterns right under their feet. The river, although it had already become frozen by the time of the Intercession of the Theotokos holiday, felt alive under their feet, strong, eternal, bottomless. There, where its floor was to begin, the starry sky began. And both above their heads and below their feet distant stars and planets circled in the loops of their melodies and sang that God's world is like Easter and that Ukraine is a bee-hive (*and people are people*).

The children walked and swimming up to them and looking straight into their eyes through the thick ice were pensive mermaids, large playful fish, blue-eyed underwater birds, red turtles, emerald water roosters, and yellow-green and marble lions. And mom and dad could be seen among them. They smiled at the children, tried to cheer them up, talked about and showed them something pleasant, yet rather vague. Little Ivan rested his head on Markus's shoulder and shut his eyes while listening attentively to his father's words (*Kyiv is a large, painfully beautiful, though unkempt, city*). And then he opened them, because he became really interested (*the father was telling the son the history of the Sviatoshyn-Brovary line*), and how and why the metro functions. Then they flew above the Kyiv region. Ivan Iehorovych saw Kolonshchyna, and Havronshchyna, the hamlet Poroskoten (*the literary mecca of the local forests*), and both the Nearby and Distant Da-cha.[31] Later, almost falling asleep, he laughed when he saw the plumber Vasyl and Mr. Petrakis, both shitfaced, looking for the Remington 870 "Wingmaster" in Petruchcho's weapons collection and being unable to find it. Then they gave up, had another drink, and fell asleep.

Lida, in an icy glow, entered a store as big as a palace and just couldn't understand how it was possible for a huge whale (*and Jonah was in the belly of Tolia the dolphin for three days and three nights*) to swim indoors. A fantastic helicopter, the black bee of the people's fury, prophesized that Oleksii would live a long life and gave Mariana and Lesia a *chervonets* for a rainy day and a hundred million Syrian pounds for a good day.[32]

They didn't get upset when they woke up in a small, short house with a huge oven. They spent the next half year, up to June, by the fire pit of that monstrous, yet warm, creation of people's imagination. They managed to get by and, thank god, they stayed alive. Turns out the old man had enough of the yellow-grey millet (*if you have food, then bad times are less bad*), and every two weeks the large head of the mare brought homemade bread and milk. Oleksii and the girls wanted to somehow strike up a conversation with it for the sake of politeness. It spat on the snow, took off its hat and yelled in such a manner that none of them tried to establish relations with that head anymore.

The children did not leave the house during the day because, for several days in a row after the search (*a looking for, a searching, a seeking*), those same good neighbors that left them for certain death were now trying to find them. And, most likely, not because they wanted to apologize to them. In the evening, when darkness and the endless, daily, and diligent snow would block the access of any strangers to the homestead, the children would come out into the starry world and run to the small inflow of the river (*three willows hung over it*), where Markus kept his fish traps made of woven willow branches. They examined these traps and played among the willows.

By springtime, the old man had sewn a bag for each of the kids.

"Why are you sewing them?" little Ivan would ask.

"I am sewing them for you," the Pilgrim would answer, "I've got nobody else."

"I don't want a bag, it's too big for me," the little boy would say. "Give it to Oleksii. Let him have two."

"One is enough for him," the old man would smile and carefully place his fat, weathered and very warm palm on the boy's greyed head (*a crooked, grey stain, from the nape to the forehead, remained until death*). "You'll go to Kyiv in the summer. You'll get by on alms along the way. So, these bags will be useful to you then."

"So, people will give us food?" the boy would ask just as he thought of it.

"Some will, some won't, but you must thank everyone anyway and keep on going."

"Will you come with us, old man?"

"Unfortunately, not."

"Then I am not going anywhere either. Let the older ones go while I stay with you. You have millet, milk, and you know a lot of tales. That's all I need."

Ivan would climb onto the hearth where the five brothers and sisters sat. The old man would smile and continue to sew. On one long and warm evening at the end of May, when all the other kids were falling asleep, Markus would instruct Lida and Oleksii:

"I'll get you to the road, God give me strength, and I'll show you where to go. You'll go alone. Don't tell anyone the truth about your parents. Tell them that they died of a disease and that you are going to your uncle in Kyiv. And forget about your last name for good if you haven't forgotten it already."

"What uncle?" Oleksii asked sadly. "We don't know anybody there."

"I'll give you an address, memorize it, they'll give you shelter for a bit. After that, you are on your own."

"Why are you chasing us away? We are good kids, we help around the house, and later we'll be able to take even better care of you. I wash the floor every day and do the dishes; I can do laundry and I know how to sing."

"We are very good kids. Don't chase us away," pleaded Oleksii.

"First of all," the old man shook his head, "they've searched for you in the village, I told you about that. And if they'll find you here—which will surely happen if you don't leave—who knows what they could do to you. Secondly, God has only given me enough strength until June. Just enough for me to feed you, to sew you some bags, and get you on the road."

"And what will happen to you later?" Lida asked.

"Later, I'll pray, lie down here on this little bed, and die," Markus answered humbly.

"Wouldn't it be better if you went to Kyiv with us?" Lida embraced the old man's right hand and rested her head on his knee.

"Like I told you," the old head gently smiled, "I was supposed to die back in March. God kept me alive for your sake. Because you couldn't have made such a trip in the winter. And now, by October-November or, in the worst case, by Christmas, you'll make it to Kyiv. God will help you because he loves voyagers and refugees of all ages and pilgrims of all religions."

"And how about kids who trek over Ukraine by foot?" "Of course, he especially likes them. C'mon, let me sing a song for you, lie down here on my bed."

"How about you, old man?" Lida sleepily muttered.

"I still need to pray until morning. You lie down, too, Oleksii, close your eyes," the old man covered the children with his winter coat and made the sign of the cross.

"How will we get by in Kyiv alone?" Lida asked barely audibly and, together with Oleksii, fell asleep. Grabbing each other's hands, they flew above the fields and forests, moving faster and faster. A large black-orange bear circled above them and yelled: "Ukraine is a beehive, a beehive."

"Sleep, my dear ones," Markus looked thought a small window at the glow of the bright stars flickering above the endless steppe. Kyiv is nice in early autumn. The leaves fall and it is cool and quiet in the valleys. And there are no bad people in Ukraine, because Ukraine is a beehive and bees don't steal, they just provide. Although, of course, people are people. Sometimes they need to be taught. And every new president is better than the previous one. And every day carries us to a meeting with God. And Ukrainians die on both sides of the Dnipro River.

In the warm days of November, lazy and stunningly beautiful Kyivites will somehow stroll along the Obolon shoreline and not one of them will be forced to think about the war.

Sven's Way, or Swan Lake

Little dolls came to the ball,
A beautiful gown on every doll.
The one in pink—the prettiest of all:
Everyone at her beck and call!
　—Sophia Andrukhovych, *Felix Austria*

Every Night and every Morn
Some to Misery are born.
Every Morn and every Night
Some are born to Sweet Delight,
Some are born to Endless Night.
　—William Blake

Habinsky was returning from the Heroïv Dnipra market, and three liters of famer's milk warmed his memory-stirred soul. The sun shone brightly, and he had no desire to go down into the metro. He walked and thought about that tale of love and honesty that took place yesterday. And what an evening that was. Not everyone gets to experience such sublimity and naivety in relations.

The pleasure that Ole-Luk-Oie gave him yesterday still waded somewhere below his belly-button and circled in a very thin, brightly-hot flame along his spine. Only one thing made him nervous: around 3 am Haba had fallen asleep and, when he awoke an hour and a half later, there was no Ole next to him. Outside the window, the workers that were removing trash from KarmaTown were yelling. Someone's car alarm was tensely wailing. The tops of trees could barely be seen swaying through the balcony doors. The fast-moving Obolon clouds floated above Kyiv, but it was difficult to follow them. The smell of alcohol, cigarette ash, and yesterday's burnt coffee filled the room. On a tiny table by the bed there sat an almost clean ashtray with two or three cigarette butts in it, half of an orange, and a pack of cookies. He felt around him and found no one. The bed was cold and a bit damp (*because the Dnipro is so close, even in very cold weather, white frizzy frost covers the steps of the metro*). He felt his throat getting dry. He went to the clothing rack and there were no women's clothes there.

"Ole?" he yelled. He shuffled barefoot over to the kitchen and opened the door. The MR and Ole were sitting at the table, drinking tea, and laughing. When they both turned around and he met their glance (*ironic and wise*), the world began to wane in Haba's eyes, the floor and the walls of the apartment swam and crashed into the darkness together with the metro station and a chunk of the Dnipro shoreline.

And it was this moment in particular that bothered our scholar a bit, both in a cerebral and cerebrospinal sense, because of its obvious inexplicability. Because it was clear that there is no way that Ole can see the

MR—because Ole is real, while the MR is the opposite, and Habinsky—is nonetheless a rational person and can distinguish between the two. But the only existing proof this morning that he had not just dreamt up that celebration of love was a tiny silvery needle (*Johanna enters with a fake headdress made up of gold rings, needles, combs, and nets*),[1] which he found by the mirror in the bathroom. So, what was it, Haba thought to himself, smiling at the sun's radiance flooding his eyes with an apricot warmth, and how is that possible? If she did indeed leave, then why did she leave behind this beautiful object that is used for pinning up hair in the form of a two-pronged little fork? Aha, I know, Haba laughed. Maybe it is to let me know that she surely will return!

"She will return!" he once again smiled out of delight and felt himself coming back to life. To a real life. Maybe he won't have any prospects but is that what is truly most important in life? If, let's say, she wasn't here, if, let's say, I only imagined her, then, regardless of that, where did this pin come from? Habinsky slyly smiled at the sun and the wind. No one can fool a person if that person does not fool himself! This slivery object is definite proof of the reality of love. But then why did Luk-Oie leave without saying bye? And why so early?

Yesterday, he was great in bed. A real Bacchus. For he is Bacco (*Caravaggio, c. 1596*). He loved her to the point of insanity, when blood hums sweetly in the nighttime expanse filled with sour cherries. So, things weren't lining up, but Haba was not too worried about it. In the lives of refugees, many strange things take place.

Having seen the sacral building of KarmaTown, Haba smiled at it as if at a living being. And, suddenly, he felt like stopping by his work. To run into The Beautiful and the Beneficial just for a minute, to catch the smell of the tender delicate onion, to touch the dry and clean root vegetables and pre-washed carrots, to see the sugar in crunchy packets, the various types of pasta, the nuts, and the bitter chocolate. To listen to those relaxing musical compositions that are always played in market's rooms. They're so pointless, so stupid, they (*maybe, precisely for that reason*) are filled with the warmth of fresh pastries, with the aromas of various meals prepared by the chefs of The Beautiful and the Beneficial and are ready to-go, these melodies go well with the bitter and lasting aroma of craft beer that is poured from morning to night at The Beautiful and the Beneficial, with the suppressed clamor of shoppers and tellers, their smiles, their small talk, their faces radiated by the light of a thoughtful choice, perhaps the first one they have ever made.

Should I get some cookies, or something else, how about some sausage, or maybe sour cream? A bottle of vodka? Cognac? Salmon? Caviar? It's so hard to make a choice. But, on the other hand, if you can already tell the difference between Chianti and Sontsedar,[2] then you can keep on going Swann's way or, better yet, Sven's.

And who is Sven, Haba suddenly thought to himself. His memory was increasingly playing tricks on him. Is it that Turkish-German dude, who sells high-end cheese in Obolon? No, it is more likely the name of the elk in *Frozen*. And there were also: Sweyn I Forkbeard, Sweyn Godwinson, Sven Kramer, Sven Yrvind, and Swen Dure.[3] There have been many Svens in this world. As it turns out, Habinsky had always wanted to have a second name. And if he were to have one then let it be Sven. It's a very simple and nice name for a simple person. Moreover, for one that belongs to the sub-category "Simple Person Refugee."

Let's say Thomas Vinterberg[4] enters The Beautiful and the Beneficial and says: "And who is that moving between the aisles with a cart of sugar and potatoes? From the way that he moves I can tell that he is a person that is intelligent, educated, simple, and a refugee, but does he have a name?" "Yes," the workers of KarmaTown answer in a choir, "that's our Sven—the northern elk, cold heart, frozen eggs, the son of Snow Bee, the lover of René Descartes and of King Shubin the First, an old coal mine monster with the nickname 'The Good.'"[5]

"Oh," says, Vinterberg, "yes, I see, just make sure you tell him that the rifle that he hid at the beach, in the woods by the water, will undoubtedly be found and this will cause a lot of problems. The people of Europe will say that he is a terrorist in which case he'd be better off being a cat-skinner and a Czech studies specialist."

Sven Habinsky quietly smiles, moves his cart closer to the Danish director, and says: "I am but a simple refugee with a cart, yet here's what I will tell you, Mr. Vinterberg. Certain people here are trying to convince me that I killed my lover's husband. Others—like my bright mind—laugh (*and cry*) at this, because it is clear that this did not happen, because this could never have happened. Not only am I not capable of killing a person, I am not capable of killing even the memory of a person. Regarding those huge bags with the samovars and authentic Russian shoes; that accordion and the Russian dolls; that coalminer's strong spirit and phallus that lost erection in a coalmine full of heavy, black dust and helplessness; and

that fear and love of a blue-eyed little lady who was simultaneously funny and horrifying, there is only one thing
I can say: this was all made-up by my new, pro-Ukrainian
memory, more precisely, by Hermes ibn Trismegistus, an
old *kobzar*, moron, and drunk. It would be better for us to
forget about him and pretend that he never existed in this
universe. Because there is no other manner of bringing
him to consciousness.

Vinterberg grabs a bottle of whiskey off the shelf,
which extends into the endlessness between the Minsk
metro station and the Cardinal Lemoin metro stop, opens
it and offers it to Sven. Drink up, boy, he says, spring
has come, beauty has come, see the water drip. A young
Kozak feels the need to set off on a trip.[6] Sven accepts
the bottle and takes a big gulp, clean as a teardrop. Then
he stays silent for a minute and checks out the light that
is coming through the large windows. He smiles again.

Maybe I did kill. Why should I argue? Maybe that's
how it was, and I just don't remember it. On the other
hand, I don't only not remember it, but I also don't remember, for instance, the battle between David and the
uncircumcised Goliath. And this, of course, does not
mean that it—that important battle—did not take place.
The whole history of mankind, these potatoes and this
fabulous sugar, these raisins and sweet-smelling oranges, which remind every conscious refugee so much of
apricots, are witnesses that this important battle really
did take place. Because, of course, if the Israelites hadn't
been victorious back then, we'd have no chance today.

Why do you think so, Vinterberg asks. Well, it's obvious. It's all about analogies. Goliath comes from a line
of giants-rephaites, he was almost ten feet tall. A true

Siberian, special forces, infantry. And countering him was this little guy, David. A farmer and ox-herder. Five thousand copper coins hung on the Philistine-giant, while David was garbed in something his brethren had patched together and paid for before sending him off into the zone of action, one which has not been designated as a war.[7] Saul, a solid colonel, perhaps also a veteran of the Soviet-Afghan war and of the Revolution of Dignity, put an American bullet-proof vest on him, but it was too heavy for our boy. The weight pulls him down, so he sits down on the ground, and says: fuck this. I'll grab my grandpa's sling, my mom's *motanka* doll,[8] and my dad's Parabellum gun. Before the contest, I'll watch a few of my favorite Federico Fellini films, read Umberto Eco, and drink a cup of coffee. And off he went, and he arrived. Goliath sees David and starts laughing. He says, who do you think you are, what's all this that you've brought along to a fight with me? With a petty rock and your comical, weak anger?

You come at me with a sword, spear, and shield, David then says and gets the *motanka* doll from his armpit, and I am coming after you in the name of the Lord of Hosts, the God of the Israeli armies. Today the Lord will give you unto me (*the motanka turns into a fantastic beast with three eyes and six wings*) and I will kill you, and I'll chop off your head and give your corpse to the heavenly birds and the earthly beasts. Let the whole world know that there is a God and that there is truth! Let European society know that the Lord saves not with the sword and the spear, and that this is the Lord's war! And he will give you unto us.

Thomas gulps down the alcohol, too, sits on the floor next to Haba, between the culinary section and the pub, and becomes pensive. This is all great, my friend, but what does any of this have to do with that rifle on the beach?

Because, replied Habinsky, here, on the third floor, in restaurants and fast-food joints, in various shops and meeting halls, in miniature quirky zoos, by the ping-pong tables and by that pool with Femida, I always see the guy that I so-called killed, along with his long-dead friends. And although Sosi is gone, I see her, too. I see many of those that are no longer with us. There are many of them and they are happy. They have all survived somehow, Mr. Vinterberg, moreover, they came here, to me, Sven Habriel Habinsky, an honest and circumcised (*although not willfully*) person, to this, as God is my witness, holy city. But this cannot be, because this is not right. Because all these whiskeys and cheeses, these artisan breads, and this wonderful Spanish wine were not made for this, the Obolon skating rink was not built so that this guy, who should be peacefully and resolutely lying in the ground together with his samovars, would be the one who is skating upon it.

Of course, many dead and many living come to the supermarket, Vinterberg agreed, animals meet the faces of people and people meet the faces of animals, but what can you do. That's the way it is these days. I agree, Sven nods, that's the way it is these days. But I need to go see Petro Petrakis and tell him about my meeting with Ole. That's a good idea, says Vinterberg, smiling. It would be worthwhile to ask Petro for her phone number, he advises, for some reason none of us thought of that yesterday.

Oh, yes, Sven says joyfully. After a wonderful night spent with a woman, every proper fella, moreover one that is hoping to finally find (*establish, open, begin, break,*

cancel, heal, psychiatrist, St. Paul, Saul of Tarsus) a social circle in Kyiv, should be the first to call his sweetie. Sensing
gratitude and joy, you should impart your most sincere
respect and deep love for her, and say other good and
appropriate words. It is recommended that you allude to
the existence of eternal love and adoration in the onto-
logical space. Point to the light in the depths of the chest
that widens; and to the bones of the skull that move, sing,
and dance under your skin; to the future that lies before
all who have ever been in love in an emerald milky way
path that begins above KarmaTown and extends into the
spiral center itself. The girl needs to be informed about
the MR. Even if the latter seems to be a real being, it is
not, because it, in essence, is only a fortuitous and illuso-
ry reproduction of the head of that mare that is tumbling
along Europe's paths and carries within it the vast and
eternal Ukrainian world.

***

The security guards at the entrance recognized Haba
and greeted him. The cashiers also smiled, followed him
with their glances, and began to energetically chitchat
about something, laughing out loud. Fine then, let the
girls laugh a bit. Employee's entrance. Second floor. And
here's Petro Petrovych's office. Habinsky knocked and
looked inside. Petrovych was sitting at his massive desk,
behind him in locked transparent cases hung rifles, an
old passion of Petro. If you're a military man, then you'll
love the tools of death for the rest of your life. Or they'll
love you. And across from him sat some chick who was
smiling pleasantly.

"Excuse me," Haba said, gazing with dry eyes at the familiar figure, "Why don't I just wait outside for a bit."

"No worries!" Petro Petrovych yelled. "Come in, Habinsky, Marta Oleksandrivna and I have just finished. Also, I need to talk to you."

"Thank you, Mr. Petro," Marta Oleksandrivna smiled at Petrovych, "I trust that there won't be any complaints about me on your end." She gave Haba the stink-eye and contemptuously pursed her lips before exiting the office.

"Who was that?" said Haba after the door closed behind her.

"Good Lord, Habinsky," Pertrovych shook his head, "that's Marta, our new coworker from the culinary department, you met her a week ago. What's the matter with you? Is it your head again?"

"Aha," Haba acknowledged, "new coworker." And he looked at his own trembling fingers. They were too long for a man who pushes a cart full of sugar and potatoes daily.

"What does your psychiatrist say? What are your prospects?"

"Exceptional," Haba shrugged, "in other words, good."

"I wanted to ask you why you haven't yet gotten in touch with my nephew? Would you prefer that he call you first?"

"Nephew?" Sven raised his eyebrows.

"Jeez, buddy," Petro Petrovych stood up, opened a closet, poured himself some whiskey, walked up to Habinsky and patted him on his back. "I don't get you. I had asked you to help Kolia Lukin, my nephew, with his philosophy exam. They moved here from Crimea, and the boy is a bit nerve-wracked. PhD studies are very important to him, he is a good student, but he needs to take the philosophy exam in Ukrainian. Do you understand the situation? You've been promising to call him for three weeks now..."

"Kolia Lukin?" Haba repeated.

"Yep, that is correct." Petrovych took a sip of whiskey and glanced at his watch.

"You mean Ole-Luk-Oie could just be Kolia Lukin?"

"Dear friend," Petrovych smiled patiently, "I don't know what Olia you are talking about, but I have only one nephew and I am like a father to him. Do you understand?"

"Yes, I remember, he is an orphan and that is why, since childhood, he was supposed to work on tomás de torquemada and michelangelo antonioni,[9] in order to protect himself from bad people."

"I know nothing about torquemada," Petrovych became gloomy. "But, I repeat, he has a PhD exam any day now and you promised to help him prepare for it. Your Ukrainian has gotten so much better over the past year—holy cow! You speak like a real person now, like a goddam *Anatomically modern human*, like the unsurpassed *Homo sapiens sapiens*. And philosophy, as far as I know, replaces neurons in your brain. Capisce?"

"Yes, I understand," Haba nodded, "ok, no problem, we can start anytime. Maybe today, maybe tomorrow, or better yet—yesterday. Yesterday's day is better suited for philosophical studies. Somehow, both the teacher and the student feel more natural when everything has been lived through already, new senses don't arise and cannot arise. You just sit on the balcony, drink whiskey, and gradually figure out the way it is."

"Alright then, so he'll call you today. Get this thing started already."

"Fine," Habinsky said, got up and, as always, began looking over the rifles that hung in translucent cases on the wall.

Never before his move to Kyiv did weapons attract him, but once he ended up in this wonderful city, he could not take his eyes off a nice rifle, if he should come across one. Haba didn't remember exactly when this happened but, either way, Petrovych noticed Habinsky's interest and started trying to convince him to join him on trips outside the city. He began describing and demonstrating what happens to a bullet when it shoots out of a muzzle and flies, full of radiance and light, into the target it has chosen for itself. And, after Petrakis and Haba truly became tight, they would travel far outside of Kyiv almost every week and go shoot at various air balloons right in the forest—blue, red, and gold. Vasyl the Inventor would inflate them and set them off on their way towards their destiny. The balloons slowly flew up and quivered, penetrated by the sun's radiance, and then just flew and flew. It turned out that the scholar was an ardent marksman. As Mr. Vasyl pointed out, the fact that he was always squinting suited him quite well when he shot. And it emphasized his defenselessness and intelligent character.

"It's good that you are not looking at what you are shooting at," Mr. Vasyl said, "that's how it should be done."

"But I'm guessing it's better to aim before you shoot, no?" Haba said, embarrassed.

"Shooting while looking at what you are shooting at—anyone could do that. But hitting the target without even imagining what it looks like—now that is the task of a true marksman."

Habinsky placed his palms on the stained glass. It was cold.

"By the way," Petrovych also stood up, "a rifle of mine that was at my dacha went missing after that time that you, Vasyl, and I were there. Do you remember? It was on your birthday. Back in November. That is, I'm not sure exactly when this happened and I'm not implying anything, but it seems to me that, on that day, I didn't touch the rifle." Petro became quiet and pensive. "And then, you see, a week later I noticed that it's gone. And I recalled that we searched for it with Vasyl. You should be able to remember. The three of us, perchance, drank all day in Kyiv and then took a taxi there. Do you remember the dacha?"

"What dacha?" Sven wrinkled his brow.

"In Publiieve-Neronove," Petrovych patiently repeated. "You don't know, by chance, where it could be? That is, not the dacha, but the rifle. I searched and searched for it...And then I remembered that you woke up first, made coffee for Vasyl and me, turned down some hair of the dog, and went home. And that's why I'm asking. It's not that I suspect you of anything, but, nonetheless, what can you tell me about this?"

"Remington 870?" Sven shrugged. "Pump-action with an under the barrel magazine?"

"Yes," Petrovych said.

"Breechface located in the front part of the breechblock, steel barreled, eight-cartridge magazine located under the barrel?"

"Yep," Petrovych confirmed.

Sven was thinking and remained quiet.

"Nope," he finally said. "Haven't seen it for a long time."

"But we shot it a few days ago. Remember? You really liked it. You said it was awesome, like a pink doll. That it was no rifle, but a doll."

"You know something, Petro," Habinsky, flummoxed, threw up his hands, "My head is not right. Today I'm diggin' this girl and then tomorrow, for instance, it suddenly turns out that she isn't a girl but a male student from Crimea, whom I, thankfully or not, never saw (*more likely—thankfully*). And this is strange, because, as you know, for my entire life I've maintained one and only one orientation—the metaphysics of Aristotle. And it concerns..."

"The thing is," Petrovych interrupted, walked up to the doors, opened them, and carefully looked right and left, "that it is the type of rifle, as far as I know, with which three weeks ago Piven and Khrobak were killed. Have you heard of them? Former cops. Rebels from the other side. It's quite the big deal. All the news websites wrote about it. Haven't you read about it?"

"Are you kidding?" Habinsky smiled. "Me and news websites? Listen, Petro, maybe it would be better if I told you about my latest meeting with the Mare's Head?"

"Once again, these were your guys, from the East," Petrovych looked squarely into Habinsky's eyes, "they were on the other side and then moved here, and, as is often the case, immediately found a job and support. And they both got shot. They say that one afternoon some Ukrainian-speaking boy, about forty years old, entered an almost empty bar, where those weirdos liked to hang out, and began reading Shevchenko out loud. They say he read with great passion."

"What a clown," Haba said, "perhaps he's a big fan of poetry. What are we talking about, Petro? These days every third guy is a clown. How about, instead, I tell you something new about Romeo and Juliet, you haven't heard this yet."

"And then this boy," Petrakis stubbornly continued, "pulls a rifle out of his jacket and shoots both. Bam-bam. Can you believe it?"

"Aha, that's what it is," Haba said in a bored voice, "fucking Ukrainian *tarantino* shit, yep, that's it. Don't read the news, Petro, you'd be better off reading Baudelaire, like I've told you many times."

Petrovych once again poured some whiskey, walked up to Haba, and once again looked into those dense, cinnamon eyes, where no emotion was visible except for a big, almost beyond-human exhaustion. He shook his head and returned to the couch.

"You understand, I already submitted a statement to the police about the lost rifle, exactly, by the way, a week before the latest killing. Everything has been officially prepared and filed. My hands are clean. Plus, I have friends in law enforcement. So, I'm not really all that worried about all of this. But you should think about it. Especially because they say that yesterday, somewhere on Iaroslaviv Val, another guy from over there was murdered. Moreover, it was with that very same rifle. And his life story was sad like that of the previous guys. He fought for the other side. Well, what can you say, shit happens. Everyone makes mistakes sometimes. Later, he came over here and everything was ok with him. He even hung up a blue-yellow flag in his car as a true sign of the transformation or metamorphosis of his soul that he had suddenly undergone. And that's the whole sad story."

"Well, I always said that they don't like refugees in Kyiv," Habinsky decided not to leave and sat down on a stool in front of the table. "How about pouring me some whiskey, too? Please, Petro Petrovych, just a half a pour. I'll have a quick drink and then I'll go. I've got big plans for tonight. I'd like to read the entire *Don Quixote* tonight, in Lukash's translation.[10] You can't even imagine what a treat that is for a true polyglot."

"Fine," Petrovych agreed, "as you wish. Just a half a pour, and that's it."

"Of, course, when have I ever drunk more than that?"

They sat there for another fifteen minutes. They chatted about the absolute necessity, on the one hand, but also the obvious recklessness, on the other hand, of drinking alcohol excessively. About the fact that spring arrived early in the city this year. About the particularities of treating springtime colds. Throughout, Haba was thinking about how milk, unfortunately, doesn't go well with whiskey. Then they bid farewell and he left his jar of milk in Petrovych's office. Drink up, my friend, drink up and be healthy. In return, Petro Petrovych handed Habinsky a white envelope, the latter shrugged, silently put the envelope in his pocket, turned around, and left. Petrovych closed his office, went outside, and smoked for about three minutes looking out into space. Then he dialed a number and said:

"Kolia, make sure you call him tonight, because he's always confused and forgets everything. And go meet with him tomorrow. You'll get philosophy, and aesthetics, and Hegel along with the Mare's Head."

Upon opening the white envelope, Haba saw a stack of green bills and a photo of a guy he didn't know. Life is so short, you know, it goes by so quickly, that it's impossible to get to know everybody in this world. But had he seen him? Yes, of course, he's seen him, he would see him, maybe, even a bit too often. Almost every day. Like, for example, when Haba shaved in the morning, brushed his teeth, or drank water from the sink at night, while staring with sadness and hope into the dark, heavy mirror.

The night arrived without dreams. Instead of re-reading Cervantes, Habinsky spent the whole evening drinking coffee on the balcony, smoking and, for some reason (*this whole story is coming to an end*), he could not stop thinking about precisely this. How does Petrakis know that it was with that rifle of his that was stolen that those three refugees, those unlucky easterners, those innocent casualties of war metamorphoses, were killed, if he doesn't have that rifle anymore? Something is fishy here. As is the case with Ole-Luk-Oie, who, as a female PhD student in the Pedagogical Department of Chernivtsi University, left behind a hairpin, and who, by the very next day, turned out to be an unfamiliar boy from Crimea (*by the way, who's to say that by tomorrow the boy won't transform into a divine turtle or into a butterfly the color of a fresh lemon*). Or how about the fact that just yesterday (*and there can be no doubt in this*), when Habinsky was drinking cognac with Ole-Luk-Oie, it was during a beautiful, long Kyiv autumn, while today, in that very same city, such a mighty spring is blossoming that before us arises (*it cannot but arise*) the question of the winter that has suddenly disappeared, or has fallen through the cracks between worlds or, perhaps, is just waiting for us, let's say, right after spring? Let us use our brains, dear friends.

If a bullet shoots out and flies somewhere, and then arrives and lands somewhere, then how do you know that it was fired from that very same rifle that you no longer possess? And that nobody possesses anymore. Can a rifle just dive into virtual non-existence? Easily. If you don't have the weapon from which the shot was made, then you don't have anything. And there is nothing to talk about. You're just giving a lot of attention to non-existent things. Don't worry, we'll figure this out. Let's say, old buddy, that we have two, or even three, dead bodies (*and spring came right after fall, which leads us to conclude that it's really winter now*). And this is a fact. But even way back then Aristotle noticed that there is no sense in facts.

Habinsky was not an expert in criminology, he was just thinking and trying to maintain a sound mind. Actually, if you really break it down, then how can you be sure that the bullet flew out at all? These flies that arrived in the mother of all cities of Rus´[11] under the cover of a dark night, or perhaps the cover of an equally dark day, could have been carrying these bullets within themselves since birth. These bullets were given to them by their mother through their umbilical cord (*if by their father—then through the phallus*). Honestly, from the scientific side of things, this version seems to be the most thoughtful and conceivable.

Just like that stubborn fact that he, a simple refugee (*this only came up today*) was being taken advantage of all this time. This is very, very sad. He was messed with by his best friends, these insidious Kyivites, cunning and all-powerful, like a cat that plays with a bird that has fallen from a tree (*neither father, nor mother*).[12] And all of its wings are broken, and its heart is in pain. And, really, no one is to blame for this. In essence, it has always been like that: Habinsky's main problem is Habinsky himself.

But it was so well thought out! Exploiting as a killer for hire a person who doesn't remember anything, is confused about everything, is not sure of anything, and will never figure out whether he shot, while reading Shevchenko, using bullets of such-and-such caliber, or didn't shoot at all.

And it would have been appropriate. Water flows into the blue sea, bang, bang, bang, and it doesn't flow out, bang (*that one, finally, in the head*), A Kozak seeks his fate, bang, bang, bang, but he has no fate[13] (*the body crumples onto the floor*). The gloomy bartender looks at the dead, at the puddles of blood that are forming on the floor, at the tired yet inspired shooter, and quietly becomes agitated.

But then suddenly help comes to the killed. Haba jumps from his stool, flies in the air and yells: "The days go by, the nights go by, the summer goes by, it shimmers!"[14] They begin shooting only in the moment that Habinsky is able to hide behind a huge mechanical piano, a large metal monstrosity that people call a pianola. Our shooter does not yet fire back, he is unable to because he is a pacifist, and he suffers from neurasthenia. He needs to make sure that everything possible and impossible has been done to find peace and good neighborly relations.

I didn't touch you, he screams, I'm a simple *kobzar*, blind and broken by fate, recall the faces of your parents (*the Bradis Table*) and may God be with you! And here, of course, those three who were hiding in the storeroom, begin blasting their revolvers. Habinsky realizes that there is no other way out, that there needs to be an escalation of conflict (*who will come here with a sword*).[15] And, in order to somehow add a culturological sense to the process, he recalls Mandelshtam. Oh, golden fleece, bang, bang, bang, three bullets—all in the heart, where are you, golden fleece?[16] Bang, bang, bang. Two more fell.

His eyes are squinted because Habinsky is unable to shoot otherwise; his hands shake. Just looking at him, any investigator would understand: if this person did indeed shoot at Piven and Khrobak (*Laurentius with his tweezers, the chandelier clinks and dings*), about whom he does not remember anything now, then it was only because he had something else in mind. And the bullets whistle (*you await me and don't sleep in a children's bed*).[17]

The pianola was struck by the last round coming out of the rifle. It started playing the dance of the little swans. Yellowed leaves, eyes lower, bamts, bamstuh, bamtsan, bamtsen, bamtsung, thoughts slumber, the heart sleeps, *Zugzwang*—it ricocheted. Haba shoots without opening his eyes and, finally, he begins having a dream. But throughout this dream—which is full of brown, yellow, and orange colors, the colors of red beets, fresh potatoes, and Egyptian oranges—he continues to thrash his enemies with lines that are damaging because of their genuineness. And everything fell asleep, and I don't know whether I am alive or just living, or if I wander along the world's path, because I no longer cry, nor do I laugh...[18] Bamtsven, bamtsaring, bamtsiudoi, bamdzen. The adversaries collapse. The pianola rattles, the swans no longer really dance (*fuck this, boys, one of them screams, this is bullshit*), but rather scatter along the stage and eerily hiccup out of fear and exhaustion.

Picking the right moment, Habinsky rolls away from behind the pianola to the oak bar stand. The attackers crawl through the windows. Haba checks his ammo, there's not much left. But to each cap pistol bullet a word can be added, overfilled with metaphorical and lethal strength. Haba has nothing to lose. Everything is clear. Captain Petrenko has died. Major Vasyl lies lifeless between Podil and Obolon, and between his calloused fingers the pages of this novel begin to grow. And there is no one left.

And Habriel stands up. The concert has concluded, buran-dada-dada, just the echo—a deception.[19] The end of all—death, budu-budu-buden, mysterious and unknown. The enemies cover the floor of the establishment with their limp bodies, Habinsky walks out of it with his pink doll (*with an under the barrel magazine*) onto the street. Your final ammo is sweeter than your last love.

Both happiness and sorrow—all of this, all of this, all—will pass, like a phantom. Four snipers simultaneously shoot in the chest the Hero of Ukraine, Habriel Bohdanovych Habinsky. God is now laying me, ti-i-i-in, ti-i-i-in, ti-i-i-in—like a violin into a case.

He slowly and beautifully rests upon one knee. He remains like that for some time, taking a break. Blood flows down his chest, soaks through his clothes, and begins to drip onto the floor. Haba places his hand on the damp shirt, looks at his hand, sagaciously and sorrowfully smiles at the doves—that is, the swans—who have shit themselves out of fear, as well as at the tearful audience (*the female ones*) seated in the arena of life.

Bid farewell, he says, missies. Missies-pixies. I've done all I could. Let those that come after me clean up after themselves. He lies down on the stage and folds his hands onto his chest. He thinks for a moment. And then utters to the vividly bright blue and yellow sky above him. I know that I cannot sleep. I know that tomorrow everything will begin again. Once again, something will begin, about which I have no idea right now. It seems like I will never-ever be able to exit this labyrinth. Once I heard a saying. There is no road back and we've already been ahead. That applies to me. Habinsky laughs, cries, laughs again, closes his eyes, and finally allows himself to enjoy the dream.

***

"Hey, son, you plan on sitting here for much longer? The film finished a while ago. Got to go home." Habinsky woke up and saw a hazy, short, dark figure in front of him.

"Okay, okay," he said, got up and looked around the hall which, indeed, was empty. "So what time is it?" he asked.

"Eleven."

"Wow," Haba muttered, "thanks," and set off for the exit.

"The exit isn't that way," the employee patiently pointed out, "you need to go this way and make a left."

"Okay, thanks," Haba went where he was told to go.

He stepped outside. A thick snow lazily falls from the sky. There's a strong wind. The streetlamps sway. Cars drive by, blinding the eyes with their headlights. He crossed the street. Behind him now was the large shopping center, that looked like a green boat, and its movie theater, which Habriel would always visit on days like this, to escape from life. And he is unable to remember its name for the umpteenth year in a row.

Somewhere nearby there is a building in which he and his wife rent an apartment. Hold on. It's this one, most likely. Turn here, and turn here. There's the entrance. The elevator slowly goes up. The doorbell is black. Its melody is barely audible, or maybe, not audible at all. It seems that the doorbell is not working, and never did work, but his wife always opens the door when he presses that black button. It doesn't matter whether the doorbell works or not. A tired Snavdulia opens the door and smiles at Haba.

"Did you have a nice stroll?" she says, helping him take off his jacket. "Did you go to the movies?"

Haba nods and heads for the kitchen. There, he sees Ferdinand, who is sipping tea. On the table are some cookies, chocolates and a dessert bowl filled with candied nuts. Having seen Haba's figure, his friend rises.

"So, I figured I'd drop by to see you, but you're not around," he smiles. "Greetings! We need to make a few interviews with famous people for our journal. Would you like to do it? I want to discuss the general strategy for these materials with you. Besides that, the boss wants you to think about a cycle of essays. The pay is good," Ferdinand smiles warmly at Habinsky, while Habinsky looks at Ferdinand with no particular expression. "And you do remember," his friend continues, "that we're having you over on Sunday, yes? But, for God's sake, please arrive before six, before the others show up, ok? So we can chat a bit. We haven't had a good sit down in ages."

Haba says nothing in response, leaves the kitchen, goes to his bedroom, takes off his clothes and, naked, slides in under the comforter. The bed is old and squeaks. The sheets are cold. The pillow is icy.

"You better go now, Ferdinand," Habinsky hears the words of his wife, "He doesn't feel very good on days like this."

Ferdinand's response is inaudible. The door slams, he has left. The wind blows through a small crack beneath the window. It needs to be patched up. Snavdulia brings in some tea.

"What did you see?"

"I don't remember," Haba says, he sits up and takes the tea from his wife. "Maybe some sort of Hollywood flick, but it doesn't matter."

His wife sits next to him, petting his head.

"My poor rabbit," she says, "my poor little head."

"I am not a rabbit," Habinsky says, "I am a lion."

"A lion-rabbit," Habinsky's wife continues to pet his head.

"Tell me the truth," Haba asks, "am I a good person?"

"You are a good person," his wife kisses his shoulder, "very good."

"And will the war ever end?"

"Of course, it will end."

"And will I ever recover?"

"Well, you've almost recovered already, it's just that you occasionally have relapses. Don't worry. The professor said that everything will pass. We should have left the city earlier. If we had left earlier, you wouldn't have had this. It's our fault. But everything will be good. Everything will pass."

"Everything will pass," Haba repeats pensively and takes a few sips. "But please tell me. Have I ever worked in a shopping center in the vegetable and sweets department? Did I ever stock sugar, vegetables, and other such things there? Maybe not this year, but last year? Perhaps before the war? Think about it."

"You better lie down," his wife gently smiled, "lie down, my love. You never stocked vegetables, never worked in a shopping center. Everything will be okay. I'll turn off the light and you close your eyes—nighty-night."

"And what will you be doing?"

"What do you mean?" Snavdulia smiles and begins to undress. "I'll lie next to you and sing you songs."

"And everything will pass?"

"Yes, my love, everything will pass."

Haba closes his eyes.

"You promised to sing something," he reminds her.

"Yes," she says, "just a minute. And what song would you like to hear?"

"'Lili Marlene,'" Haba replies.

"Okay," says the wife, "okay." And she remains quiet for a few minutes. The song of the wind outside the window is a lovely match for her silence, together creating a certain peacefulness.

"Begin," Habinsky says, "right from the chorus."

"Okay," and then his wife once again stays silent for some time.

The wind blows (*it's winter, my brother, winter*).

"By KarmaTown," the wife finally begins, "in the light of the lamppost," her voice is not strong but rather very tender, gentle, "a flock of crows circles. It's Kazimir, it's shamisen, it's our frontier, it's Swann, it's Sven," Haba starts falling asleep, jumps out of bed and flies some-where into time and space, "My Lili Marlene, My," Sna-vdulia repeats (*kissing Haba in the forehead*), "Lili Marlene."

***

He woke up at night. His wife slept next to him, the wind whirred, and it was very cold in the room, but that is not what caused him to open his eyes: that doorbell that never rings—it rang. It rang so quietly that Haba was the only person in the whole world that could hear it. Habinsky glanced at his wife's face. She slept as sweetly and soundly as a child. Careful not to awaken her, he got up and went into the adjoining room. The doorbell was singing, and it sang a very delicate little song. "There is a high mountain," it sang, "and below it is a meadow."[20]

Habinsky went up to the door. He felt that, if he would open it, he would never be able to fall asleep again. And if he didn't open it, he would never awaken. He took a breath and closed his eyes. He opened the door—and almost broke into tears. At the doorway stood five tiny children (*sleep, little Jesus, sleep*).[21]

The End, August 2018

Notes

Introduction

1   For an analysis of Russophone culture in Ukraine, including
    Volodymyr Rafeyenko's Russophone works, see Marko
    Puleri, *Ukrainian, Russophone, (Other) Russian: Hybrid Identities
    and Narratives in Post-Soviet Culture and Politics* (Berlin: Peter
    Lang, 2020).

2   For analyses of the Revolution of Dignity and the Donbas
    war see Serhy Yekelchyk, *The Conflict in Ukraine: What Everyone
    Needs to Know* (Oxford: Oxford University Press, 2015); Serhii
    Plokhy, *The Gates of Europe: A History of Ukraine* (New York: Basic
    Books, 2015); Olga Onuch and Gwendolyn Sasse, "Maidan in
    Movement: Diversity and the Cycles of Protest," *Europe Asia
    Studies*, Volume 68 (2016): 556–587; Taras Kuzio, *Putin's War
    Against Ukraine: Revolution, Nationalism, and Crime* (CreateSpace
    Independent Publishing Platform, 2017); Marci Shore, *The
    Ukrainian Night: An Intimate History of Revolution* (New Haven:
    Yale University Press, 2018); Mychailo Wynnyckyj, *Ukraine's
    Maidan, Russia's War: A Chronicle and Analysis of the Revolution of
    Dignity*. Ukrainian Voices 1 (Stuttgart and Hannover: ibidem,
    2019) and Paul D'Anieri, *Ukraine and Russia: From Civilized*

Divorce to Uncivil War (Cambridge, Eng.: Cambridge University Press, 2019).

3   Volodymyr Rafeienko, "Iak mova vyznachaie pamiat'. Konspekt rozmovy z pys'mennykom Volodymyrom Rafeienkom u L´vovi u ramkakh Misiatsia avtors´kykh chytan´. Moderuie Marianna Kiianovs´ka," *Zbruch*, August 19, 2019, https://zbruc.eu/node/91540.

4   *Seven Dillweeds*, a mini-novella found in *The Length of the Days*, and translated into English by Marci Shore, appeared in 2017 in *Eurozine* (https://www.eurozine.com/seven-dillweeds/).

5   Rafeienko, "Iak mova vyznachaie pamiat´."

6   Volodymyr Rafieienko, "Volodymyr Rafieienko, avtor knyhy 'Mondegrin': 'My vse shche rostemo, i dai nam Bozhe kolys´ nareshti vyrosty'," interview by Oleh Kotsarev, *Yakaboo*, June 3, 2019, https://blog.yakaboo.ua/rafeenko/.

7   See Yuliya Ilchuk, "Hearing the Voice of Donbas: Art and Literature as Forms of Cultural Protest During War," *Nationalities Papers*, Volume 45, Issue 2 (March 2016): 56–273; Nazar Kozak, "Art Embedded into Protest: Staging the Ukrainian Maidan," *Art Journal* 76 (Spring 2017), no. 1: 8–27; Tanya Zaharchenko, "The Synchronous War Novel: Ordeal of the Unarmed Person in Serhiy Zhadan's *Internat*," *Slavic Review*, vol. 78 (2019), no. 2: 410–29; and Alessandro Achilli, "Writers, the Nation, and War: Literature Between Civic Engagement, Trauma, and Aesthetic Freedom in Contemporary Ukraine," *Modern Language Review*, Volume 115 (October, 2020), no. 4: 872–90. The Birkbeck School of Arts and the University College London School of Slavonic and East European Studies held the forum "Depicting Donbas: Creative and Critical Responses to the War in Ukraine" on April 25–26, 2019. The Ukrainian Studies Program at the Harriman Institute, Columbia University organized the conference "Five Years of War in the

Donbas: Cultural Reflections and Reverberations" on November 1–2, 2019. A video recording of that conference can be found at https://harriman.columbia.edu/event/conference-five-years-war-donbas-cultural-responses-and-reverberations. The forthcoming Spring 2022 (vol. 9, no. 1) issue of *East/West: Journal of Ukrainian Studies* will be a special issue featuring articles from the Columbia conference.

8   For example, Iryna Tsilyk's 2020 film *The Earth Is Blue as an Orange* won the Directing Award for World Cinema Documentary at the 2020 Sundance Film Festival and Valentyn Vasianovych's *Atlantis* (2020) was Ukraine's official selection for best international film for the 2021 Academy Awards and a prize winner at the Venice Film Festival. International exhibitions that have given attention to the Maidan and the Russian-Ukrainian war include *I Am the Drop in the Ocean* (2014, Kuenstlerhaus, Vienna, curated by Alisa Lozhkina and Konstantin Akinsha), *Permanent Revolution: Ukrainian Art Today* (2018, Ludwig Museum, Budapest, curated by Alisa Lozhkina and Konstantin Akinsha), and *At the Front Line: Ukrainian Art 2013–2019* (2019, Mexico; 2020, Canada; curated by Svitlana Biedarieva and Hanna Deikun). See also Mark Andryczyk, "Vlodko Kaufman's *A Conversation* at the Ukrainian Museum," *Harriman*, Fall 2020, http://www.columbia.edu/cu/creative/epub/harriman/2020_fall/vlodko_kaufmans_a_conversation.pdf.

On Essence

1   Here, and from now on, in parentheses are Habinsky's observations (author's note).

2   This paragraph is a parodic quote of the song "Chto takoe
    osen´" ("What is autumn") by the Russian group DDT, that was
    very popular just after the fall of the Soviet Union. Here the text
    is presented in a Ukrainian translation that extensively and
    playfully jumbles the original text (translator's note).

3   A-Ba-Ba-Ha-La-Ma-Ha is the name of a prominent Ukrainian
    publishing house founded in 1992 by the poet Ivan Malkovych
    (b. 1961). Originally focusing on children's books, it now
    publishes for a wider array of readers. Malkovych borrowed
    the firm's name from a fin de siècle short story by Ivan Franko
    (1856–1916) entitled *Hrytseva shkil´na nauka* (Hryts's schooling),
    in which that string of syllables is used by a boy to learn to read
    in the Ukrainian language. A "baba" is a grandma in literary
    Ukrainian and a "chick" or "babe" in Ukrainian slang. Both
    Franko and Malkovych hail from Western Ukraine (tr.).

4   A *halychanka* is a girl from Halychyna (Galicia), a region in
    Western Ukraine. A *pannochka* is a term used in Western
    Ukraine to refer to a young lady. The writer Leopold von Sacher-
    Masoch (1836–95), who wrote in German, was born in the
    largest city in Halychyna, Lviv. The term "masochism" is derived
    from his name. Lviv is known as the "City of the Lion" (*Misto
    Leva*, from *lev*, meaning "lion" in Ukrainian; tr.).

5   Andrii Kokotiukha (b. 1970) is a writer popular in contemporary
    Ukraine (tr.).

6   A pun on the colonial reference of Kyiv being "the mother
    of all cities of Rus´," See also note 11 in "Sven's Way, or Swan
    Lake" (tr.).

7   See note 2. This is another subverted translation of that DDT
    song (tr.).

8   Mystets´kyi Barbakan (The Art Barbican) and Kupidon (Cupid)
    are two Kyiv bars popular with the city's creative circles (tr.).

9   *Tini zabutykh predkiv* (Shadows of forgotten ancestors) is
    a 1911 novella by Ukrainian writer Mykhailo Kotsiubynskyi
    (1864–1913). It was the basis of a 1965 film of the same title by
    Georgian director Sergei Parajanov (1924–1990) (tr.).

10 This a reference to the term "Russian tourists," which was used
    by Russian separatist leaders to excuse the presence of Russian
    soldiers in Ukraine who were there supporting separatists in
    the Donbas. The term was later mocked by activists when they
    "occupied" the Russian pavilion at the 2015 Venice Biennale (tr.).

11 A *molfar* is a person in the Hutsul culture of Western Ukraine's
    Carpathian Mountains that purportedly possesses magical
    powers (tr.).

12 St. Cyril's Church is located in Kyiv and is part of St. Cyril's
    Monastery. In 1787, it was closed and its living quarters were
    converted into a hospital. Later it was transformed into an
    insane asylum. The church was restored in 1750–60 by the
    Ukrainian architect Ivan Hryhorovych-Barskyi (1713–1785),
    who incorporated elements of the Ukrainian Cossack Baroque
    architectural style to its exterior. In the 1880s, Mikhail Vrubel
    (1856–1910) painted murals in its interior, which otherwise
    remains mostly in its original, medieval style (tr.).

13 "Junta" is the term used by Vladimir Putin to label and
    demonize the pro-European Maidan activists, which led his
    vassal, Ukrainian President Viktor Yanukovych, to flee Ukraine
    for Russia (tr.).

14 *Nepozbuvna benteha* was a meme that was very popular in
    Ukraine in 2017, after translator Oleh Korol used the phrase
    when translating the phrase "concrete feeling of excitement"
    in John Fowl's 1965 novel *The Magus*. Korol's use of a new
    Ukrainian word combination (or his revival of a forgotten one)
    was heralded by many as being an example of the vitality of
    the Ukrainian language and highlighted the importance of

actively translating into Ukrainian to ensure the language's continued growth. However, there was also a backlash that criticized its use for trying to find a phrase that is uniquely Ukrainian. The latter view resisted efforts of de-russification that were accelerated since the Maidan and the Donbas war. In social media throughout 2017 the phrase became a lightening-rod for debates over the need, twenty-five years into Ukraine's independence, for the existence of a Ukrainian language free of the constraints and russification that it was subjected to in Soviet times (tr.).

15 The author knows that formally it should be MH. But let's just keep it as MR (author's note).

16 This is a reference to the 1895 poem by Lesia Ukrainka (1871–1913) entitled "Pivnichni dumy" (Midnight thoughts) (tr.).

17 *Surzhyk* refers to a mixing of Ukrainian and Russian languages that is spoken in some regions of Ukraine and in nearby regions of the country. There exist different types of *Surzhyk* that reflect social and historical developments in the country's regions (tr.).

18 *Varenyky* is a Ukrainian word for pierogies (tr.).

19 From the 13th century Old French prose romance, *Vulgate Cycle* (tr.).

20 The *bulava* is a ceremonial mace. It was first used as a weapon in Eastern Europe and became a symbol of authority. In Cossack-era Ukraine, in was held by its leader, the hetman and, in today's Ukraine, by its president. A *pirnach* (*pernach*) is a small *bulava*. A *bunchuk* is a tug, or long pole with horse or yak hair at the top. It was adopted by the Slavs from the Turco-Mongol khanates (tr.).

The Beautiful and the Beneficial

1   The name of the supermarket references the 1955 poem by
    Maksym Rylskyi (1895–1964) entitled "Troiandy i vynohrad"
    (Roses and grapes). The poem concludes with the lines "Human
    happiness has two equal wings: // roses and grapes, the
    beautiful and the beneficial" (tr.).

2   Roshen is the brand name of the very profitable chocolate
    and candy company owned by Petro Poroshenko, who was
    the President of Ukraine from 2014–2019, when this novel
    was written. The name of the company is the middle part of
    Poroshenko's last name (tr.).

3   The original words used here—*slid* and *poslid*—are part of a play
    on words in Ukrainian. *Poslid* can be "poultry litter," "placenta,"
    or mistakenly, "diarrhea" in Ukrainian, while *slid* means
    "trace" (tr.).

4   In Ukrainian, *vyrii* denotes the warm south to which migratory
    birds fly before the fall of winter (tr.).

5   These lines are from "Bidna moia zh holovon´ko" (My poor
    little head)—a poem written by Ivan Mazepa (1639–1709),
    Hetman of Ukraine in 1687–1708, which also serves as the text
    for a popular folk song—and "Shcho po horakh snihy lezhat´"
    (When snow lies in the mountains), which is an old *chumak*
    (salt-trader) folk song (tr.).

6   Bankova Street in Kyiv is where the Presidential Administration
    of Ukraine is located (tr.).

7   Kobza is a Ukrainian folk instrument of the lute family,
    traditionally gut-strung, with a body of a single block of wood.
    A player of kobza is called *kobzar* (bard), who was often blind
    and sang dumas (Ukrainian epic poems or ballads). The term
    itself is of Turkic origin (tr.).

8 "Because we love the work // that transforms into creativity"
   is a line from the Maksym Rylskyi poem "Roses and Grapes"
   mentioned in note 1 in "The Beautiful and the Beneficial" (tr.).

9 *Boh ne telia, bachytʹ zvidtilia* is a traditional Ukrainian saying
   that means that all of one's deeds in life are witnessed by
   God (tr.).

10 This is an old Ukrainian saying, *Iazyche, iazyche, lykho tebe
   klyche* (tr.).

11 Until 2018, the Ukrainian-Russian war in the Donbas, which
   began in 2014, was officially referred to as an Anti-Terrorist
   Operation (ATO) by the Ukrainian government (tr.).

12 A pun on a popular Ukrainian drinking song "Hei, nalyvaite
   povniï chary" (Hey, fill the glasses), which has the line, "let our fate
   not forsake us" (tr.).

13 This phrase is a quote from part VI of Ivan Franko's 1905 poem,
   Moisei (Moses). The translation of the complete poem by Vera
   Rich can be found here: http://sites.utoronto.ca/elul/English/
   Franko/Franko-Moses.pdf (tr.).

14 Among Haba's offerings are *pliatsok*—the name of a pastry-pie
   or cake that is baked in western Ukraine and is rather exotic
   in most other regions in Ukraine—and *chokoliada*—a western
   Ukrainian term for the literary-Ukrainian *shokolad*, both
   meaning "chocolate" (tr.).

15 *Banosh* is a cornmeal dish popular in the Carpathian region
   of western Ukraine. *Zupa* is the western-Ukrainian word for
   "soup" (other regions of Ukraine use the term *sup*, which is
   pronounced [soop]) (tr.).

16 This is a quote from the 1859 poem-anecdote by Stepan
   Rudansky (1834–1873) entitled "Prosʹba" (A Request) (tr.).

17 "Nie ma sprawy" means "no problem" in Polish. Nestor
   Makhno (1888–1934) was an infamous Ukrainian anarchist

revolutionary, who was commander of an anarchist army in Ukraine from 1917 until 1921 (tr.).

18 This phrase is from the Ukrainian national anthem (tr.).

Sosipatra

1 In the original Ukrainian, it is *Patre ty moie patrane*, which is a language pun. The Ukrainian language has the vocative case (which the Russian does not) and the author plays with it here as part of his frequent play with, and discovery of, a new language. *Patra* in the vocative case is *Patre* (O Patra!), while *patrane* is something that has been gutted, like a chicken or a fish purchased at a market (tr.).

2 In the original it is *pishla porokhom petrom oleksiiovychem*, which is a reference to Petro Oleksiiovych Poroshenko, who was President of Ukraine at the time of the writing of the novel. Poroshenko is sometimes referred to by the nickname Porokh, which means "dust" in Ukrainian (tr.).

3 Vasyl Stus (1938–1985) was a poet and Soviet dissident who lived and worked in the Donbas. He died in a Soviet forced labor camp. There was a movement in 2008 to rename Donetsk National University in honor of Stus, but that initiative was eventually rejected. After the occupation of Donetsk by pro-Russia rebels at the start of the Donbas war, the university relocated to Vinnytsia and was renamed in honor of Stus. Meanwhile, a commemorative plaque for Stus on the old university building in Donetsk was removed by the pro-Russia rebels (tr.).

4 *Kolhosp* is the contraction of the Ukrainian phrase for the collective farm (*kolektyvne hospodarstvo*), known as *kolkhoz* in Russian (tr.).

5   Aleko is also the name of the chief protagonist in the 1827
    narrative poem *Tsygane* (The Gypsies) by Aleksandr Pushkin
    (1799-1837), in which an outlaw escapes his native city and
    moves to a Gypsy camp, where a tragic romance ensues (tr.).
6   Viktor Yanukovych famously misspelled the word "professor" as
    "proffesor," among other mistakes, when listing his academic
    rank on the Central Election Commission CV form in 2004,
    registering himself as a candidate for President of Ukraine. For
    many, this served to confirm the dubiousness of his declared
    academic merits. Yanukovych fled Ukraine for Russia during
    the 2014–15 Revolution of Dignity (tr.).
7   Mykola Samokysh (Nikolai Samokish, 1860–1944) was a painter
    in the Russian Empire and in the Soviet Union. He was of
    Cossack descent. He had many ties to Ukraine and illustrated
    books of stories by several Ukrainian writers (tr.).
8   Heqet is an Egyptian goddess that has a human figure and
    a head of a frog. She is the goddess of fertility and creation.
    A shamisen is a popular Japanese string instrument that
    features a long neck (tr.).
9   In the original, this phrase is written in Russian and stands out
    from the rest of the text, which is in Ukrainian (tr.).
10 Right Sector is a nationalist paramilitary organization formed
    during the Maidan/Revolution of Dignity. It later became
    a political party. *Russkii mir* (Russian world) refers to a concept
    heavily propagated by the President of the Russian Federation
    Vladimir Putin, and his proponents, that proclaims that
    there is a broad Russian civilization beyond the borders of his
    country that needs to be diligently nurtured and defended from
    its enemies. It is a concept that he invoked to justify his illegal
    annexation of Ukraine's Crimea, his invasion of the Donbas,
    and other neo-imperialistic Russian ventures (tr.).

11 "Katiusha" is a very popular Russian Soviet military march from World War II that is based on a folk song (tr.).

12 From the Russian Soviet WWII song "V zemlianke" (In the trenches) (tr.).

13 This is a fragment of a comical Ukrainian folk song (tr.).

14 Haba says this in Russian, which stands out in the original. It is also from the song "V zemlianke" (tr.).

15 The phrase "In your prayers, nymph, remember everything for which I am guilty" appears in Russian in the original and stands out from the rest of the text (tr.).

16 In the original, this phrase is in Russian and stands out from the rest of the text in Ukrainian. It comes from the very popular WWII-era Russian Soviet song "Sviashchennaia voina" (The sacred war) (tr.).

Conditionalis

1 "The Butterfly Dream" is the most famous story in the Zhuangzi (ca. 3rd century BC), one of two foundational texts of Daoism, along with the Daodejing. It has the line: "Once Zhuang Zhou dreamed he was a butterfly, a butterfly flitting and fluttering around, happy with himself and doing as he pleased. He didn't know he was Zhuang Zhou" (tr.).

2 Klavdiievo-Tarasove is a town that is located northwest of Kyiv (tr.).

3 In this exchange, Tarasove refers to Taras Shevchenko (1814–1861), Ukraine's national poet (tr.).

4 Another reference to the Zhuangzi story. See note 1 in "Conditionalis" (tr.).

5 Another reference to the Zhuangzi story. See note 1 in "Conditionalis" (tr.).

6   Another reference to the Zhuangzi story. See note 1 in "Conditionalis" (tr.).

7   From the Ukrainian folk song "Zapaliu ia kul solomy" (I'll burn a sack of straw) (tr.).

8   Mykola Lukash (1919–1988) was one of the 20th century's most prominent translators into the Ukrainian language (tr.).

9   Volodymyr Sosiura (1898–1965), Mykhail´ Semenko (1892–1937), Ivan Drach (1936–2018), and Ivan Franko (1856–1916) were all prominent Ukrainian poets (tr.).

10 Another quote from the song "V zemlianke" (tr.).

11 This line is from the Vasyl Stus (1938–1985) poem "Meni zoria siiala nyni vrantsi" (A star shone upon me this morning) (tr.).

12 Quattrocento is a term that refers to Italian culture of the 15th century (tr.).

13 Ressentiment is a psychological state of self-abasement that comes from repressed feelings of hatred and envy (tr.).

14 Yellow and blue are the colors of the national flag of Ukraine (tr.).

15 The *tryzub*, a trident, is the state coat of arms of Ukraine (tr.).

16 In Ukrainian, the word *perspektyva* has the same meanings as the word "perspective" in English: as in "a way of seeing things," or in the sense of graphical projection in art. However, it also has a figurative meaning in Ukrainian that is close to the English "prospect," as in "to have a bright future ahead of you" or "to have potential." The author plays with these various meanings of the word in Ukrainian from this point on in the novel (tr.).

17 This is a line from the 1849 poem "Sotnyk" by Taras Shevchenko (1814–1861) (tr.).

18 Ambrogio Lorenzetti (c. 1285/1290–1348) was an Italian painter who experimented with perspective.

19 A *piven'* is a "rooster" in Ukrainian, while a *khrobak* is a "worm" (tr.).
20 This sentence lists several traditional, clichéd Russian clothes and other objects (tr.).
21 This is an adjusted quote from the poem "Skify" (The Scythians) by the Russian poet Aleksandr Blok (1880–1921), with this novel's author adding the word "Russian" to the original line (tr.).
22 "Across Russified cities" is a line from a Ukrainian song written by Kostiantyn Moskalets (b. 1963) and made famous by singer Taras Chubai (b. 1970). "And you didn't come again today" is from the well-known Russian song "Kolokola" (Bells) (tr.).
23 In the original, the dictionary's title is *Slovnyk ukrains'koï movy*, which has the acronym SUM. The word *sum* means "sadness" in Ukrainian. Thus, in this manner, "sadness" was present at Haba's party, too (tr.).
24 This is a reference to Taras Shevchenko's well-known poem "Reve ta stohne Dnipr shyrokyi" (The mighty Dnipro roars and bellows) (tr.).
25 This is a line from the poem "Baliada pro tin' kapitana" (A ballad about the captain's shadow) by Bohdan-Ihor Antonych (1909–1937) (tr.).
26 A *sopilka* is a Ukrainian fife, usually made of wood (tr.).
27 Another line from Antonych's poem "Baliada pro tin' kapitana" (tr.).
28 A popular Ukrainian song "Stoït' hora vysokaia" (There is a high mountain). Text by Leonid Hlibov (1827–1893), music by Mykola Lysenko (1842–1912) (tr.).
29 From song seven of the 1862 narrative poem *Velyki Provody: Poema (1648)* (The great farewells: A poem [1648]) by Panteleimon Kulish (1819–1897) (tr.).

30 From Panteleimon Kulish's 1899 narrative poem *Marusia Bohuslavka* (tr.).

31 Poroskoten, a village outside of Kyiv, is where this novel's author once lived. Nearby Dachi and Distant Dachi is a play on the names of the Blyzhni Sady and Dalni Sady parts of the Dachnyi Masyv, which is near Poroskoten (tr.).

32 In pre-revolutionary Russia and in the Soviet Union, a *chervonets* was a golden coin of three, five, or ten rubles. In the Soviet Union, the ten-ruble bill was often also referred to as a *chervonets* based on the bill's red color (tr.).

Sven's Way, or Swan Lake

1 From the dramatic etude *Ioanna—zhinka Khusova* (Joanna, the Wife of Chuza) by Lesia Ukrainka (1871–1913) (tr.).

2 A Soviet sweet red wine that appears in many Russian literary works (tr.).

3 Swen, Svein, Sweyn, Swen, Sven, or Swenn is a Scandinavian masculine name. Sweyn I of Denmark (916–1014), also known as Sweyn Forkbeard, King of Denmark (963–1014); Sweyn Godwinson (1020–1052), was the eldest son of Earl Godwin of Wessex, and brother of Harold II of England. Sven Kramer (b. 1986) is a Dutch long skater; Sven Yrvind (b. 1939) is a Swedish sailor; "Young Swen Dure" is the title of a Scandinavian ballad (tr.).

4 Thomas Vinterberg (b. 1969) is a Danish film director and co-founder of the Dogme 95 movement in filmmaking. Among his films are *The Celebration* (1998), *Submarino* (2010), *The Hunt* (2012), *Far from the Madding Crowd* (2015), and *Kursk* (2018) (tr.).

5 Shubin is a mythological spirit of the mines whose legend lives on in Donbas mining towns and cities. He can be good or evil.

He is also a figure in today's local pop culture. The Donetsk-based brewer Sarmat brews a beer called Good Shubin (tr.).

6   This is a line from the traditional Ukrainian springtime song "A vzhe vesna, a vzhe krasna" (Spring has come, beauty has come) (tr.).

7   See note 11 in "The Beautiful and the Beneficial" (tr.).

8   A traditional Ukrainian doll that is believed to keep evil spirits and ghosts away from children (tr.).

9   Tomás de Torquemada (1420–1498) was Grand Inquisitor of Spain and a major figure in the Spanish Inquisition. Michelangelo Antonioni (1942–2004) was a celebrated Italian filmmaker who was very influential in art cinema. The names are written in lower-case in the original text (tr.).

10   See note 8 in "Conditionalis" (tr.).

11   "The mother of all cities of Rus′" is a phrase from the *Primary Chronicle* by Nestor, in which it is ascribed to Prince Oleh who thus made the city of Kyiv his capital. Given Russian claims to the heritage of the Kyivan Rus′ since the imperial times, the phrase retains a colonial tone for many Ukrainians (tr.).

12   In Ukrainian, the original phrase *ni bat′ka, ni nen′ky* ([she listend to] neither [her] father, nor [her] mother) is a highly recognizable quote from Taras Shevchenko's 1838 poem *Kateryna* (tr.).

13   Parts of Taras Shevchenko's 1938 poem *Dumka* (A thought) are interspersed with the words "bang" in this sentence (tr.).

14   A line from the Taras Shevchenko 1845 poem "Mynaiut′ dni, mynaiut′ nochi" (The days go by, the nights go by) (tr.).

15   This phrase is from the film *Aleksandr Nevsky* (1938) by Sergei Eisenstein (1898–1948). In the film, Prince Aleksandr Nevsky of Rus′ addresses the knights of the Teutonic Order after their defeat by saying, "Who will enter here with a sword, will perish from a sword." The film had clear anti-German allusions and

was used in the Soviet Union for propaganda purposes before
and during WWII (tr.).

16   There are references here to Osip Mandelshtam's (1891–1938)
poem "Zolotistogo meda struia iz butylky tekla" (A river of gold
honey poured from the bottle, 1917) (tr.).

17   A line from the song "Temnaia noch´" (Dark night) by Vladimir
Agatov (1901–1966) from the Soviet film *Dva boitsa* (Two fighters,
1943) (tr.).

18   A line from the Taras Shevchenko 1845 poem "Mynaiut´ dni,
mynaiut´ nochi" (The days go by, the nights go by) (tr.).

19   This paragraph and the following one feature quotes from
the 1932 poem "Amin´" (Amen) by Bohdan-Ihor Antonych
(1909–1937). For more translations of Antonych into English,
see Antonych, Bohdan-Ihor, *The Grand Harmony*, translated
by Michael M. Naydan (Lviv: Litopys, 2007) and Antonych,
Bohdan-Ihor, *Night Music: Selected Poems*, translated by Stephen
Komarnyckyj (London: Kalyna Language Press, 2016) (tr.).

20   From the popular Ukrainian Song "Stoït´ hora vysokaia" (There
is a high mountain). See note 28 in "Conditionalis" (tr.).

21   A line from the Ukrainian Christmas carol "Spy, Isuse, spy"
(Sleep, little Jesus, sleep) (tr.).